WAKING UP AT REMBRANDT'S

WAKING UP

AT

REMBRANDT'S

A NOVEL

THOMAS LLOYD QUALLS

WAYFARER BOOKS
SAN JUAN MOUNTAINS, COLORADO

WAYFARER BOOKS

SAN JUAN MOUNTAINS, COLORADO

All Rights Reserved
First Edition Published by Lucky Bat Books, 2013
FIRST EDITION TRADE PAPERBACK 978-0984693627
Second Edition Trade Paperback Published by Wayfarer Books, 2026
Cover Design and Interior Design by Connor Wolfe
SECOND EDITION TRADE PAPERBACK 978-1-965320-91-4

10 9 8 7 6 5 4 3 2 1

WHOLESALE INQUIRIES? You can find our books available via Ingram, offered with standard trade terms and lifetime returnability. With printing bases in the US, the EU, the UK, and Australia, Wayfarer has the capability to fulfill orders globally. Our titles are available wherever books are sold in paperback, ebook, and audiobook. Find our books at local Indies, Bookshop.org, iTunes, Barnes & Noble, Amazon > US & International, or direct at wayfarerbookstore.com.

WAYFARERBOOKS.ORG
WAYFARERMAGAZINE.COM
WAYFARERBOOKSTORE.COM

For August

ONE PART

THE PAINTER

The painter folded back the heavy curtain, standing in the stream of light breaking through the damp thickness of the room. He paused, still holding the drape in his hand as he considered with suspicion that a world could exist outside the window. Then he reached for a stained cloth and tied back the opaque fabric. He returned to the easel, wading through the illuminated particles of air on his way.

To paint one must forget everything else. Where you live, who you know, what you eat, when to sleep. The landscape of the canvas becomes your only reality. The planet you inhabit is a single plane of infinite dimensions, stretched like a guitar string, and standing before you like a concubine waiting for your command.

The painter knew that color was not something you controlled but something you set free. He believed that color knew its way home. But he lived in a time and place that considered color suspect, blasphemous even. Those who worshiped color, who cavorted with it, who dared to practice its alchemy, were seen as witches. The respectable world would tolerate his kind to a point, for entertainment's sake. So long as the painter could rein in color, make it behave. So long as he painted the world the way they wanted it to be. So long as he had no thoughts of his own.

You might think of a thought as an invisible, innocuous little thing. Something that barely exists. But a thought is something hard to conceal. Hold a thought and it melts all over your hands. Touch something else and now you've left traces of it. Hide it under your shirt and it bleeds through.

The painter was not afraid of thoughts though and did not consider thinking to be risky behavior. To the painter, the only risk that existed was to stop painting. To stop trying to solve the riddle of light and dark. Or to paint what someone else wanted him to see. To tell the colors to stand up straight, form a narrow line, eat their peas. That was death.

The painter knew the mirror lied. And the canvas told the truth. A simple breakfast of beer, fried eggs, and herring. These things you could trust. Words, whether written or spoken, were barely worth sitting still for, not worth repeating. In the end there is only light and dark. And the two are not so far apart.

LOVE: STUDY 1

i am the lion and
you are the lamb and
as prophesied,

we will lie down together.
because love is greater
than the sum of its parts.
love breaks all rules,
ignores all customs,
cuts through fences,

slips across front lines,
trespasses against us,
steals what it pleases,

pleases its victims,
slays its critics,
bleeds us to delirium,

and saves our souls.
no matter the cost.
love does not keep a ledger.
love has no master.
love knows no yesterday.
love seeks no tomorrow.

love needs nothing.
and nothing can be
taken from love.

love is terrifyingly complete.
love is truth unbound.
love breaks all rules.

DILLON

The café is dark except for a pale flicker from the fireplace and the tiny halogens over the bar, leaving me just enough light to close down, but not enough to encourage visitors. The wood, oil paintings, and tapestry of the café have taken on a quiet beauty, a stillness in sharp contrast to the hustle and energy of a few hours earlier. Like the feeling after a thunderstorm, when mother nature has been brought to orgasm and then drifts off to sleep.

As I am putting up the last of the glasses from the busy evening, I hear your quiet entrance. You glide up to the other side of the bar and silently plant your waifish frame on a barstool, careful not to disturb the cafe's slumber. You rest your chin on your forearm, and your disheveled black hair hides one of your deep-set dark blue eyes, as well as the thin scar above it. Your signature slouch has taken on more of an Eeyore-esque quality than usual.

Last night you received an e-mail from a young literature student you met over coffee three months ago. You fell fast, as you're known to do, and since then she's been seen wearing your clothes to class more than once. Two weeks ago she left on some kind of ecotour. Yesterday she dumped you for a guy from Paraguay she just met. You've spent the day in a cultivated state of agoraphobia and have only surfaced because you know I'll be the only one here at this hour. For several pregnant minutes neither of us speaks.

Okay, Dillon, Don't tell me all this reflective sadness is over the girl. I finally say, instead of hello. *Something else is bugging you.*

You look up, but make no attempt to form any words in response. Though we've never shared a bed, you and I know each other better than most married couples. We've stared down the moon and talked the sun up so many times we're able to have whole conversations where not a word is spoken.

Jillian, don't belittle my grief, you begin to justify your sulking condition while I pull down two glasses from the overhead rack. But I refuse to offer much of a shoulder.

I'm just saying, you're sounding a bit provincial here. Doesn't a fling in South America fall under some exception to the rule? Aren't you holding her to some kind of puritanical standard? I place the glasses in front of you, reach up into the wine rack and select a dusty vintage.

I cut the foil and begin to extract the cork. The metaphor fits. As I begin pouring out the dark red liquid, you also open up. "It's not the fling. It's not that I can't deal with it. It's that she can't. She's turned it into more than that."

I swirl the elixir, briefly inspecting the color and then, pausing just before I sip, I ask *What did you expect? She's young. You think she could go out into the world for the first time, meet an exotic stranger, have a fling, and then know where to put it all?* I finally tilt the glass to my lips.

I expected her to talk to me about it. I mean, if she can't talk to me about it, what does that say about me? What does it say about this whole open-minded, modern-day beatnik persona I've been sporting around for years? If she's not comfortable talking to me about something as simple as a little travel fling, then who am I?

I sit staring at my wine for a minute. *I see...* I start, but then think better of it. I fill my glass again and top yours. I get up from the table and walk back around the bar to the brick oven fireplace. I pick up the long pizza spatula and swiftly slide it into the oven, retrieving a pie brushed with walnut pesto and topped with grilled veggies. With my right hand, I hold the spatula balanced on the edge of the bricks. My left hand crumbles goat cheese over the top of the pie. Then I slide it back to a deep corner of the oven, where the coals are still showing a little red and orange through the gray ash. I remove the long spatula and lean it against the bricks.

Returning to the table, I pick up my wine and hold the silence on my tongue just a little longer. Unwilling to disturb it by swallowing or letting it out.

You pretend to examine a knot hole in the polished wood of the bar. *Do you think I'm a good person?* You finally utter, looking as resigned as a question mark.

Don't be so narrow, Dillon. It doesn't fit you. I demand. *Nobody is simply good or bad.* I realize now you're grappling with the void and I'm not going to let you dwell there, if I can help it. At the same time, I know that as seamless as we are, I can't actually save you from it. The gap between one person and another is just too large sometimes.

I don't know, this sounds pathetic and trite, but I really feel like I've just been wasting my life. I've pissed away too much time in school. Too much time just drinking wine and reading poetry, changing my major every few weeks and showing up occasionally to take tests—just delaying the inevitable. I've been pretending I wasn't subject to the same rules as everyone else. You know, the bylaws of the world of jobs and spouses and cars and houses and two-week vacations. I imagined I was above all that.

But the world demands some level of respect, at least that we stay awake for it. All this time I thought I was being all Zen, that it really didn't matter what I did with my life, so long as I wasn't hurting anyone, blah, blah, blah. But lately, I don't know. I feel like I have nothing, I am nothing, and there's nothing I can point to and say: that's mine, I built that, or I'm really good at that. And now that I think about it, I'm not sure I can even say I'm a good person. In a way, how can I blame her? What do I have to offer her or anyone?

I realize it's worse than I thought. *What is Zen about focusing only on being good. Believing you are good is like believing in the half moon. I pour more wine. What would Mary Oliver tell you, Dillon... "You do not have to be good. You do not have to walk on your knees..."*

"...for a hundred miles through the desert, repenting." I know, but what if Mary Oliver was wrong?

First of all, bite your tongue. But second, what if the ascetics were wrong. What if escaping from the sensual isn't the way. What if the search for enlightenment has to embrace the bliss of the sensual. Maybe we're supposed to walk that dangerous edge between good and bad. Maybe that's the very needle we have to thread.

And wasting time? How do we judge a good use of time? And who gets to decide? You remember Rilke and the panther? How he sat and stared at it for hours or days. Until he really saw it. Most people would say that sitting all day staring at a caged panther is an irresponsible waste of time. But an artist has a completely different way of looking at the world. A resort to poetry never hurts with you.

You weren't about to give up the existential dagger so easily. *On the other side of that shiny coin, both physics and philosophy teach us that if you look at anything too closely, it disappears. That's what I've done. I stared at my life until it's virtually non-existent.* You are bent on being inconsolable.

I use the pizza oven again to buy more time. Only after I remove our dinner from its kiln, slice it, slide it onto a plate, and place it between us on the table, do I think of something. *I don't think it's that your life has disappeared. You've just realized it wasn't what you thought. Which is exactly what Rilke was doing, stripping away the illusion and finding clarity, discovering the real essence behind the mask.* You'll have to concede on this I hope, as I'm running out of metaphors and reasons to leave the table.

Before you can respond, though, I hear myself continue. *I think I get it, you feel cheated. But not in the romantic sense. Because you think she might have found something real, something which has so far eluded you.*

I know you thought your psyche was unshakable. But I think that's because you were sitting high up on the throne of your ego, instead of planting your feet on the ground with the rest of us mortals. You might be able to place some of the players in your life on the gameboard, and to even calculate your moves, but you aren't in control of the whole game. I shred some Parmesan and serve each of us a slice.

Come on Jilly, I thought we were friends. Stop holding the mirror so close. You plead with a laugh.

Okay. That bitch. I can't believe she'd do something like that to you. I lift my piece of pizza off the plate, turn it, and bite off the end. *Better?*

Thank you. Jesus. That's all I was looking for. You contemplate the slice on your plate and play with it for a minute, generally uninterested. You pick off a topping and bring it to your mouth. Nibbling like a finicky cat. Washing the bite down with a drink of wine.

I pour you a little more.

You take another sip, but it goes down wrong and you sputter and cough for a few seconds. When you catch your breath, you admit, *Ok, you're right, of course. I'm aloof and cynical. About a lot of things. And I do resent that she may have already found a path in life when I can't even seem to find a clean fork in my apartment.*

What are you going to do about it then? You can't navigate a river from the banks. All you're doing is strategizing, thinking things to death. That isn't life. It's thinking about life.

I empty the rest of the bottle into our two glasses. You hold up yours. I meet it.

After a moment, I add, *In case you've developed some sort of amnesia about the human condition, let me remind you, her life isn't going to be perfect. And neither is yours, whether you're with her, someone else, or alone. Life isn't that tidy.*

Still, it doesn't make sense to me. I thought we were good. It doesn't add up.

I can't believe you are still moping. *I thought you were listening. Life isn't math, Dillon. It isn't science, it's art.* I get up and go to the bar for more wine. This is going to be a long conversation.

WORDS: STUDY 1

words are shy creatures.
words know their names,
but they won't come when you call.

words hate bright lights.
words won't dog and pony.
they nap during the day,

and wander far from camp.
words are a border collie's
worst nightmare.

words are bashful.
to get them to the page,
you must look the other way.

you must hide yourself,
and become someone else.
words are not playdough,

words are changelings.
words are rare metals.
words require an alchemist.

PHILLIP

Tall and lanky, you straddle a bar stool leaning over a copy of Peter Mayle's *A Year in Provence*. Your spider-like fingers are splayed over the paperback cover, like a miniature flesh and blood music stand.

Generally, your belief in your own literary genius is steadfastly unshakeable. Despite your lack of discipline—you spend most of your free time reading other people's novels rather than writing your own—you've been telling us all for years that a Pulitzer is inevitable. Lately though, at the age where you are about to be pushed through the exit door of your twenties without any literary accolades, you are beginning to consider the remotest of possibilities that you have either overestimated your talent or your work ethic. And you've begun in earnest to start to think about doing something about it, like some actual writing, maybe.

Unlike your friend Dillon, you are in no imminent danger of suffering from acute self-awareness. Your fledgling insight has brought on a certain kind of paralysis, though, caused by reading your own writing on the days after you pin some actual words to paper. It is often tempting to just replace the veils of illusion once we've glimpsed what's underneath.

We all build imaginary prisons for ourselves. Believe we are trapped behind the invisible bars of the lives we have somehow carelessly constructed for ourselves, despite our youthful promises to ourselves. We see adults who are stagnant and miserable as we grow up. They graffiti the walls behind them with their mistakes and we swear secret oaths that we will heed those warnings. We're much too clever, we know all the shortcuts and the back alleys. The bad-job, wrong-marriage, mid-life, quiet-desperation monster is too slow and boorish to ever catch us. Our lives will not be wasted. We will stay young and be talented and successful and beautiful and prosperous.

Most of all we'll be *free*. We will do exactly what we want. We will be exactly what we want. A new renaissance genius. A cure-finding doctor. A Nobel Prize laureate. A fireman who rescues children from burning blazes. Or a writer who takes people out from behind their invisible bars and into new worlds.

You look at your notes. Notes and notes. Scraps of paper collected from years of your life. Some of the years barely memorable outside the little scraps of paper. Torn pieces in various sizes and shapes. Scribbles. Smeared ink on drink napkins. A line on the back of a faded receipt. A few phrases boldly written over the fine print on a parking ticket. Poems and thoughts meandering through the blank areas of envelopes. To most, they are nothing more than filler for a junk drawer or a journal. To you, they are legitimacy, freedom, self-actualization.

REMBRANDT: STUDY 1

the painter painted pictures.
his brush painted words.
the painter bought pricey antiques

and rare books which he didn't read.
the painter had no need for grammar.
words fell from his brushes

already knowing where to stand, sit, lie down.
the painter stopped thinking.
he forgot his technique.

the painter did not understand sentence structure.
and still he spoke
better than anyone has.

the precision of art is beyond philosophy.
it is beyond all science.
the painter's brush did not know how to read.

MAGGIE

Darkness has made itself at home outside. You pick up a stack of papers and read the caption to yourself: *Mercado v. State*. You set the fresh draft of the brief on top of the marked-up sentencing transcript and close your laptop.

Although you haven't cleaned it up, it's a good first draft. Or so you think. But you won't know for sure until you read it tomorrow with fresh eyes. You glance at your watch. It's ten minutes after seven. You are meeting Christophe in twenty minutes at the café. It's a short walk from your office. You have a few minutes to kill.

You decide to go ahead to the café. You rise, move to the side of your desk and push in the chair. Your hand pauses, resting for a moment on the black leather high back, as if it can't move until your thoughts do. You stare out the window like someone who has walked into a room only to realize they've forgotten what they came for. Snowflakes swirl around in concentric circles then move outside your view. More take their place. You wonder in the same floating and passing sort of way if it is actually snowing again or if the wind has merely coaxed these flakes from their resting place on your roof to perform this dance for you. You don't really need an answer, though. It's the question that comforts you.

You are tired of always answering questions, of always needing answers. Always believing all the questions have to be answered. Pretending there are actually answers. And even getting paid to convince others they're true. That there is such a thing as right answers. As the whole truth and nothing but the truth.

Despite the complexity of your work, you are convinced your brain is under-stimulated and spends all its extra time thinking up things to drive you mad. Mostly these things are questions that can't be answered. At least not with an essay-style answer. No, these answers require deep mathematical calculations, the likes of which are completely out of the grasp of someone who skirted math in favor of art, literature, and the law. Impossible riddles like the secret to long-term happiness. How to make money and still like yourself. How to reverse major career decisions. And how to tell your perfect boyfriend you're meeting for dinner in twenty minutes that you aren't sure you're in love with him anymore.

The "M"-shaped wrinkle between your eyes becomes more defined. You eye the drink of whiskey on your desk. Questions your client will ask enter the door. You pretend to ignore them as you reach for the glass.

You'll have to explain to him again how there are certain facts you can't make go away. There was a fight. An altercation. A "fracas," the law calls it. Your client was involved in the fracas. And though the entire incident lasted but a few seconds, someone died in the fight. And that someone was an undercover cop. You trace the rim of the glass with your finger.

It doesn't help that the fracas was over a drug deal. Others were involved, but your client, Steve Mercado, was the oldest, so he was successfully painted the ringleader by the State. A cop was dead and the State needed a fall guy. Other facts made your client less than sympathetic. Testimony was presented that Mercado hated the police (even though he didn't know the deceased was one), that he always carried a knife, and that he'd been shooting his mouth off the day before about taking down this dealer if he tried to screw him. It doesn't help that Mercado was drunk during the fracas. His BAC just an hour after the arrest was 0.18%, more than twice the legal limit. Playing into the State's hand was the fact that Mercado is Native American. The prosecutor used the stereotype at trial with shameless effectiveness. You lift the glass to your lips, take a sip.

Also, Mercado—angry about being caught in the politics of an election year—was less than a model prisoner during trial. And then there was the monument built to honor the slain police officer. Another shameless but effective move by the State to seal Mercado's fate. You swirl the whiskey.

Big Bird used to say there's no such thing as the way it should be.

You didn't attend the ceremony unveiling the monument, but you were told they mentioned nothing of the deceased's questionable service record. Nothing about the dozens of citizen complaints filed against him, nor his penchant for beating up people while they were in handcuffs. Not a word in the local newspaper about how even the cops on his team were wary of his increasing need to manufacture drug busts to feed his own addiction.

You'll have to explain again to Mercado that you have no idea how the court will rule. Yes, the law is on his side on a few issues. It's clear from the record that Mercado's trial lawyer did a less than adequate job.

If accused of a crime, the Sixth Amendment guarantees each of us the right to a fair trial. Now, the definition of fair trial often depends upon where you live. But the key ingredients should be: unbiased jury, fair judge, a prosecutor who doesn't hide things, cops who tell the truth, and a defense lawyer who doesn't sleep through court. Not too much to ask to keep us from living in a police state. You'd think. But a violation of those rights isn't always easy to prove. You are more likely to have a long career as a human shield in a war than you are to convince an elected judge to reverse a death penalty case. You stare into the bottom of the glass, no tea leaves.

To prove Big Bird's point, there's this thing judges use called *harmless error*. It goes something like this: With our crystal ball, we—the overseers of justice—can see into the minds and hearts of each of the twelve jurors in this case, and thereby we know that had this error not occurred, it wouldn't have made a lick of difference to any of them. It's a useful tool, this harmless error, when you are a judge who needs to avoid the political cost of doing something like reversing the death sentence of a man charged with the slaying of a police officer. Even though the law says you *should*. The decisions are written in black and white. But if you look closely there are gray watermarks behind every page.

Of course, Mercado doesn't care about Big Bird. He wants you to tell him that you're going to get him out of prison. It doesn't matter that it's a feat better suited for a Superhero. It doesn't matter that these days you are feeling less like Superwoman and more like Sisyphus. And it surely doesn't matter to him that you are faced—once again—with relationship ambivalence, with the prospect of ending what once seemed like it could finally be the one. Or that you find yourself in the position of breaking another heart and then facing the coming days and nights alone.

Big Bird has a star on Hollywood's walk of fame, you know.

The snow keeps dancing. Enticing you to forget the questions and follow its steps. Your gaze dissolves beyond the snow and for a moment, so do your thoughts. You lift the glass again.

A passing ambulance shakes you from your trance. You glance at your watch and finish off the drink. Then you set down the glass, pull on your coat, turn off the light on your desk, and go outside. You collect snowflakes on your shoulders as you make your way across the parking lot.

JILLIAN

If you've come to see me, there's a reason. Coincidence is a word we've made up to explain something we can't explain. If you've come to see me, you are thirsty. Whatever series of events led you to this street, this door, that barstool, you are not here by mistake.

Tell me your pleasure and I'll pour the best I have. We can leave it at that if you like. If you are too timid, too wary to risk more. There will be another time.

But there's no guarantee I will let this time slip by so easily. Chances are I'll push a little. It's hard to keep the door shut if someone knocks. Hard to stay quiet. Even the most reticent will usually surrender a hesitant *who's there?*

If I tell you my name, you'll have to open the door. Just a little.

It's Jillian.

Then, what can you do? It's only polite to return a name for a name. You'll surrender this one thing. A small trust will be passed. No reason to close the door again now before you have to leave. Only our names have passed between us. But you feel safe. So small a gesture, but so intimate. Like a kiss.

Maybe I'll respect the distance left between us at first. And so, feeling at ease, you might offer up a little more. Or, I may just sit quietly on my side of the bar. Sipping from my innocent looking drink. Listening to the ice shift in my glass. And, feeling the need to fill the space, you might offer something else.

Usually we'll start with something simple. Say, an observation. Something in your hands, your clothes, your face will start to talk before you do. Or a streak of blonde may fall loose from my baseball cap. You'll offer, generously, that this year belongs to the Cubbies. I'll smile a little.

People say you can tell a lot by what a person orders. But only the obvious. The stuff you don't need to wait for them to order to know. There is so much more to learn. The way people hold their drinks gives them away. And which seat they choose. Whether they ask for a paper or read the menu. Bring their own New Yorker or check the email on their phones. Pretend to wait for someone or start talking as soon as they sit down.

Cafés and bars are better than therapy. When's the last time your shrink gave you a drink before you started talking? Or a bowl of roasted garlic and tomato soup with sourdough bread.

If you come to see me, eventually we'll get to it. We'll trade stories. Share drinks. Become friends. I will listen. And I will talk. Sooner or later, you'll get what you came for.

Life isn't really linear. Although it's generally perceived that way. The stories we tell are woven like snakes around a divining rod. A center of time containing all that's ever been told and heard. Remembered and forgotten. Lost and found. Our pasts, presents and futures are unwound, stretched flat, cut into pieces and held up with human arms. In this way they are understood by a human culture who has forgotten all but a few of the numberless dimensions, a culture who has lost its sight looking for its name. So when I use the word *then,* or words like *before, next* or *after that,* please understand what I mean. Simply, what I am saying happens.

It's hard to say where a story begins and ends. You have to draw an arbitrary line somewhere. Somewhere between perception and reality. Between what is spoken and what is heard. Between what is written and what is edited out. I know this, you can't have an ending without a beginning. Even if they are really just random pieces of the middle that tend to stand out. Staccato notes on the page. Points on a circle.

There was a time when the café wasn't. Synergistically, that is. The idea was there. The dream. And after a while, so was the building. But the two hadn't come together. Hadn't become bigger than their sum.

The building was. But not as it is. Hand-cut pine, weathered stone, colored glass. It's origin is not known. Perhaps it was a government field office. Or a Pony Express stop. Or a home to a prospector stopped short on the journey west.

However it began, it stands firm today. A testament to its builders. Even though it was neglected for years. Locked up and untended. Summers and winters moved through the valley, carving new faces on the landscape. The structure stood silent and strong, unshaken. As if it were meditating. Resting. Preparing itself. Surrounding itself with wildflowers and roses.

⎯⎯⎯

It's hard to say where a story begins and ends. How the ethereal comes into words. Or when. What we know is what happens. What we hold are pictures. What we understand is action. The swing of a hammer, turn of a screw. Paint on canvas.

This can be said. It is recorded that in 1922 there was a fire in the County Clerk's Office. The flames licked the ink from many of the records there. Including those having to do with the title history and origin of the old stone building on the sunny side of the hot springs in a meadow hidden from the lakeshore. The home of untamed cats and wild roses which somehow flourished in the narrow beams of light breaking through the locked wooden shutters. A silent fortress tucked between the field of wildflowers and the sight of the lakeshore.

≡

Before the fire, though, came the Treaty. Borne of the minds of people accustomed to small rooms. The Treaty promised a certain group of natives the official return of a piece of stolen land. The land stood near a pristine lake high in the mountains. A slice of paradise in today's world, but a largely useless corner of the earth by standards of the time: unsuitable for agriculture, uninhabitable several months of the year.

This act of *returning* was confusing to the natives, who considered it impossible to own land. No matter how tightly you clinched your fist, your pen, other people. Out of necessity they entered into relationships with land, water, fire, and the invisible, threads that tie all things together. They distrusted anyone who spoke of separating and buying or selling these things like wares.

As things go, this returned property included a certain site. A handful of land hosting a mysterious field of roses and grape vines. And the stone and pine building on the sunny side of the springs.

Over time, most of the natives returned to the lower valleys. The higher slice of land remained officially theirs, but trappers, panhandlers, and loggers steadily crowded the area. The land tucked away from the lakeside became a vacant lot, with absentee owners. The building was boarded up with machine-cut wood, obscured by weeds and overgrown roses. The future café would wait and sleep.

In native circles, a talking stick is passed around a fire and stories are told. Through tales of bravery, adventure, and loss, the ghost is made real. The form is brought into words. Somewhere between the treaty, the fire, and the wine and food, the café reinvented itself. It became a talking stick.

LOVE: STUDY 2

love wears a mask.
love is in disguise.
love comforts you

as it tells you lies.
love is a candle.
love is a rose.
love is the thorn
between your toes.
love is the blindfold.

love is the bed.
love is the hard floor
when you crack your head.

MAGGIE

Besides bartending, I also manage the café and open all the mail. A few weeks ago, we received a notice informing us that the U.S. Government has decided to lease to the local Sowhas the very same land it gave to the Tribe nearly a century ago.

In July of last year, the current administration in Washington held a much-publicized environmental forum here. On the agenda was the subject of protecting and restoring the clarity of the area's large, famed, alpine lake. More than half the lake sits on what once was land owned entirely by the Sowha Indians. The closest shore of this lake lies less than half a mile from the doors of the café.

One of the agreements reached at this summit involves the return of a portion of these sacred lands to the Sowha, and grant money for their upkeep. The deed apparently covers 40 acres of lakeshore property. Additionally, the agreement grants the Tribe a 30 year lease on 350 acres of land. The very land upon which this brick and stone building sits. Which is why we were given official notice.

It's complicated, but from what I understand from talking with you, this land already belongs to the Tribe. Story goes that first time Virgil, one of the café's owners, set eyes on this boarded-up-and-forgotten piece of real estate, he immediately went searching for its owner to make an offer. The absence of County records must have daunted more than a few predecessors, but Virgil was not swayed. Eventually he traced it back to the Sowha Tribe and somehow managed to reach an agreement to lease this space.

Now, along comes the Government and wants to lease to the Tribe land that it already owns, with a provision that the Tribe use part of the grant money to create a cultural heritage center. Stranger than this, the Tribe is somehow willing to go along.

Here's where it starts making sense. There has been a change of leadership recently, and the old man Virgil bargained with those years ago has been replaced. More importantly, the grant monies come in a fixed amount, which includes a substantial amount earmarked for the purchase or building of the heritage center. Whatever grant money is not used in creating this cultural center is still the Tribe's to keep. If only the Sowha had a building already, the monies allocated for this would be a windfall.

You have experience in litigating tribal land use matters and so Virgil naturally asked for your help on this one. Right now, you're pretty much the only thing standing between an actual bowl of pine nut soup becoming a picture of one.

No more politics. you say as you fall into a seat at the bar. I slide a cup in front of you, but the coffee is still on perk. You showed up earlier than usual today and I haven't slept well in days. I need a shot before I have this conversation.

Wishful thinking. I reply.

No, you explain, *I mean I can't listen to any more of it.*

Speakin' to the choir, sister. I say, wishing I had something more to offer than a cliché, like a cup of coffee for instance. The slow drip, drip, drip taunts me.

You slouch at the bar and look as tired as I feel. The truth is, the last few years have taken a toll on everyone. I can't remember a time when people were so openly polarized over anything. It's as if the world is suddenly personal to us.

I haven't had a conversation for weeks that wasn't somehow about the collapse of civilization. It's impossible not to talk about. I can't seem to help myself. It even came up in my conversation with the Sowha Chairman a couple of days ago.

How's that going? I ask, half-afraid I'm skirting Scylla for Charybdis. But like you, I'm tired of the debate. I'm tired of hearing everything but the truth on the news.

Don't ask. You moan.

Well, let's forget about all that for now. The boys of summer are reporting for duty as we speak. Spring Training starts this week. I point to the red "C" on my blue baseball cap. If baseball isn't safe to talk about, we're done for. I look back at the coffee, again, like I am placing a call to the bullpen.

Sometimes people bring up things to talk about which are not the things they really want to talk about. Maybe we don't know exactly what is bugging us until we think it through out loud. Sometimes this throws me off, other times I'm able to see through it.

This morning, you catch me in a moment of weakness—before I've ingested anything but the smell of coffee—when the real subject makes a surprise entrance. *Do you think I'm obsessed with death?* You ask, completely ignoring my effort to take this conversation to a more morning-friendly place. I'm not sure where to go with this. Almost compulsively I turn around again. The brew pot still mocks me.

Love, what tear in the celestial fabric did that thought fly through? I beg, hoping to buy the coffeemaker more time.

Christophe said he thinks I'm obsessed with death. And therefore, I can't embrace life. Specifically, life with him, he means.

Still coming to sleepy grips with the realization that this conversation is happening before the cavalry of caffeine, I hear my voice replying, "No, just the opposite. Think about it. You're anti-war, anti-death penalty, and pro-adoption. If anything, you're fixated on life, not death." I really have no idea where that came from, but it seems to cheer you up. You smirk and an inkling of life returns to your face.

In some ways, he does have a point. I mean, between the death penalty work, my anti-war rants, and the pending death of the café, there is a theme. You run your hands through your hair. *I feel like someone stole my life sometimes, and I'm here by default. It's like a metaphysical theft.*

Someone should sue. I demand, thinking I'm still being funny. But it turns out this is not the prompt you need. I might as well hand you a wooden box to stand on. Say one that used to contain cleaning agents.

The law can't help. People need to find a way to work things out on their own. I've heard this rant before. *The profession is filled with bullies and egomaniacs. It's ill-equipped to actually fix anything.*

It occurs to me this is a conversation we'd usually have after a few drinks, not before coffee. But since I'm feeling a little light-headed anyway, I decide to play along. *Are you challenging the wisdom of a system that just recently figured out it might not be okay to execute children?*

You don't need much encouragement, though, and I realize I'm not helping as you continue your speech. *The system is archaic, stuck in the Dark Ages, and the players who fret about on the court's stage are barely able to keep their own footing. Which would be funny—in a Shakespearian way—except for the tragedy that these players are in charge of so much.*

What is it with everyone being so morose all the sudden? First Dillon, and now you. I look back once more and reach for the pot. Finally.

Coffee?

Sure. Can you put something in it? You ask.

I oblige. It is Saturday, after all. And well, I'm a bartender.

I'm not saying there aren't good intentions in the mix. It's just that, I've come to realize over the years, humans are a messed up lot. So putting us in charge of things—besides stuff like building parks and bridges—is really not such a good idea.

Second thought, I think I'll have a little something in my coffee, too.

Where are you going with this? I finally ask, more curious than accusatorial. *Is this mostly about Christophe?*

Yeah. Another one bites the dust. You reach for your cup again.

Wanna talk about it? I am a bartender, you know.

No, not really.

I pour another shot into your coffee.

WORDS: STUDY 2

words are impossible little creatures.
they won't come when you call
or call when you come.
they march out of step
and sing out of tune.
they bump against other words

and get tangled in wire.
they stray from the crowd
and get lost in the woods.
they stumble
over thoughts
and spill off the page.

PHILLIP

You sit at the bar before your shift, scribbling in a spiral notebook. I'm doing the usual prepping and polishing. I can't imagine what you are writing. I can't imagine it being any more complicated than say a grocery list or more deep than which beer you like and why. The pros and cons of breast implants?

I know you talk the talk. You quote from the Romantics, have apparently muscled your way through the likes of *Tropic of Cancer* and *Ulysses*, and you constantly have your hand wrapped around a torn paperback. But writing is wholly different from reading. For all your talk of being a writer, I've never read anything you've actually written. Eating in a restaurant is one thing, operating one is another story entirely.

Curious, I slink over in your direction. *Whatcha writing? Ode to the beautiful bartender?*

How'd you know? You ask, feigning surprise.

A girl knows these things. I say, even though I know you will flirt with anything that breathes and has developed mammary glands. Not that I haven't. Breasts or not. Then again, I seem to find beauty in obscure locations. Not that I'm interested, necessarily. The point is the writing. And what kind of trail that pen is leaving. And if I traced that trail backwards, where it would take me. I want to ask if you'll let me read it. But I know the better course is to act like I'm not that interested.

Ah, yes. I forget. You are Jillian the Omniscient. You look up for the first time, but only for a second, then return to scribbling out your thoughts. Or whatever they are.

I decide on a direct approach, sort of. *If we were in Vegas, what would the odds be that anyone besides you will read that?*

Ouch. That's no way to encourage an artist.

There should be a way to erase things we've said, to take out a giant cosmic eraser and brush away the words from the big cartoon balloon in the air. I struggle to regain my footing without looking like I've lost it. *What I meant was, do you save the writing for your romantic victims? Are they the only ones who get a peek inside that little book?*

You put the pen down. *Are you flirting with me?*

Please. I say and turn away. Then I realize this will get me no closer to my goal.

Are you trying to get into my pants so you can read my writing, or is it the other way? You ask, putting down your pen.

After a pregnant few seconds, I answer, *Okay, suppose I have a motive. Do you care which one it is?* I'm worried that I'm crossing the line here. I don't really want to sleep with you. And this could easily escalate into a sexual version of chicken.

You say nothing. It's time for you to go to work, so you close the notebook and put the pen in your apron. As you are getting up to log into the computer, you slide the notebook across the bar. *Just the last entry.* You say, looking me straight in the eyes. *That's it, okay.*

<hr>

The café is owned by two of the most interesting people I know, Virgil and Grace, who also happen to have a great love story. Their paths crossed a few times when they were younger, but the timing was never right. Until fate brought them together again a few years ago. And this time it stuck.

Virgil used his student loan monies to travel in his twenties. He carried a journal and took notes everywhere, writing down the details of conversations and colors. Eventually he turned those notes into a series of allegories which he called *The Saffron Chronicles.* The stories follow two Indian lions through their unnaturally long lives as they witness histories unfold. The books were published, and did modestly well, but they did not turn Virgil into a modern day Gatsby. The royalties helped them to buy the café, though. And their combined resources allow them to buy good wine, Irish linens, and local organic food. They also pay the staff well and leave the restaurant in my hands when they take leave, which is more and more these days.

⸺

Virgil turns the corner into the wait station. Quick on his heels is a tousled mesh of amber hair framing a pair of wide sea blue eyes. While my first impression of her is that there isn't much upstairs, I'm sure most people who meet her couldn't care less. She is unquestionably striking. Blue eyes, porcelain skin, and petite features. From the looks of things, I'm not the only one who has noticed. The rest of the servers are hanging about—sipping coffee, telling stories, tying their aprons, fixing their hair—but they all stop what they are doing to stand momentarily speechless when she turns the corner. If you knew this crowd, that's saying something.

Virgil introduces the waifish girl, *Hey gang, this is Samantha. She'll be training today with Phillip, so I want everyone to be ready to help her or Phillip out.*

Help Phillip out. Are you kidding? How much more help do you need than to have this gift dropped in your lap?

Virgil continued with his introduction. *I know I give this speech every time there's a newcomer, but please remember that she's new and I need you to back up all the lies I've told her about what a tight and efficient team we have here. In other words, try to be on your best behavior and pretend that you take your jobs seriously. Good luck Samantha, I know they're not pretty, but they're all we've got.*

Hey, I'm Phillip. You say with a confident, but friendly nod of your head.

Hi. Glad to meet you. The new girl says sheepishly as if she were being introduced to a friend of her parents.

You look nervous. First restaurant gig? You guess.

How'd you know? Is it that obvious? She asks, looking like she's worried she might have food on her face.

Well, you learn to spot 'em. Once you get the hang of the restaurant gig, you've kind of got it. Like riding a bike. You can tell when someone's not comfortable in the saddle. Just like you learn to tell restaurant people from non-restaurant people.

Restaurant people?

Yeah. Those from planet restaurant. This world kind of has its own species. You'll see.

What do you mean?

Well, I have this theory— You begin.

Oh, god. Not with this again. I moan, while passing, on the way to the kitchen.

Undaunted, you continue, *Never mind her. Like I was saying. I have this theory that restaurant people have been magnetized, and restaurants emanate a certain gravitational pull which only those from planet restaurant can feel.*

Okay. Your accidental student answers.

To begin, there are front of the house people and back of the house people. Or roughly, kitchen people and servers. All kitchen people are kind of the same. They're generally more crude and are better left in the kitchen than allowed to mingle in the front of the house.

With us respectable folk. I chime in as I return with a rack of fresh glasses. *We let Pip here live in his own world sometimes. Doctor says not to wake him up.*

Ignore her. You insist, waving your hand in my direction. *Where was I? Oh yeah, if you're front of the house, it's still best to have the back of the house on your good side. Tip them out and buy them beers after every hard shift. Trust me, there'll be plenty of times when you need them to pull you out of a jam. And they'll remember.* When Sam's back is turned you throw a stern glance my way. I return my best *who, me?* look. You go back to your pupil. *Let's go set up our section.*

What else, what else? I tease as you walk by the bar again, your new shadow in tow.

To her credit, Samantha laughs at this. But probably not wanting not to show you any disrespect on her first day, she asks how *waiters* figure into your theory.

You should probably know that the industry has changed that name to servers. I don't really understand why everything has to undergo a name change, but in fairness, we really don't do much waiting. Unless it's really slow. We're really more like liaisons between the more unruly kitchen people and the people at the tables.

Before the crowd gets here let's make sure there are enough lemons cut and silverware rolled. Since we have to borrow a knife from Jill to cut lemons, I'll move on to bartenders.

As you and your protégé approach the kingdom of spirits again, I put on my best face for her. Virgil might get upset if I run her off on her first day. I give you another innocent look, then look to the new girl, *Hi, I'm Jillian, sorry your tour guide here is a litle self-absorbed. And that you're having to suffer through the philosophy of planet restaurant. We're not all so strange.* I extend my hand.

Hi. I'm Samantha.

From her demeanor, I get the feeling she is used to women being catty with her. So I take a different tack. *Seriously, though, don't let Mr. Hemingway there put you off, we're really a pretty harmless bunch.* You sneer playfully and I stick out my tongue.

Like I was saying, bartenders, they collect and distribute jokes at will. And, they have an uncanny knack for eliciting confessions, even from non-believers. As you can tell from that one, they also have a need to have their own territory.

Don't worry Samantha, whatever brainwashing occurs today we'll find a de-programmer for you. I assure her in a mock-serious voice, not looking at you.

Then you snatch a knife and lead her away from the corrupting influence of the bar. *Pay no attention to the woman behind the bar.*

You pick up a small tray full of salt and pepper grinders and lead Samantha through the tables in the main dining room. *Of course we can't forget those that make life here possible. The people drawn to the other side of restaurant life, the eating and drinking.* You glance up from your table prep to make sure your audience is still following.

What do you call them? She asks. I can't tell whether she is actually interested or just placating you. And I'm sure you don't really care. You only care how much time and attention she will require before she'll let you coax her out of her jeans.

Funny you should ask. Yes, they need names as well, let's see there are: suits, dates, drinkers, cracker people…

Tell her about the ones we fear the most. I interrupt.

Oh yes, the rhinestone purses. *You start wiping down the vinegar and oil bottles while you continue the indoctrination. They are definitely the most feared of all. They tend to show up just before the lunch shift is ending, order minuscule amounts of food, split the tiny portions between the whole group, drink a wide variety of hot teas, hang around for hours, ask for separate checks, and leave between 12 and 17 cents a piece on their tip trays. Then they wrap up their tea bags in little pieces of cellophane extracted from rhinestone clad clutch purses, smile broadly and leave a nearly debilitating trail of perfume on the way out.*

You're exaggerating. She says at first, then follows with, *Really?*

You'll find out soon enough, but ask anyone here. Swear.

You pick up the empty tray and the hand towel and turn back to the wait station, your crimson-haired apprentice following behind. *Let's make some raspberry tea.*

As you show her where the bulk tea is kept, and things like how much water to use and what buttons to push, you continue with her education. *Running a close second are cracker people.*

Insert joke about stupid white people here. I can't help myself.

You march on, unfazed. Cracker people seem innocuous enough upon entering the planet. They usually consist of couples, often well-dressed, well-spoken, well-mannered, with a least one toddler in tow. The toddler is the defining characteristic of cracker people. As far as I can figure out, cracker people are just happy to be out of the house. Perhaps this is why they will do virtually anything to secure the child's entertainment so they can have some semblance of a normal evening out.

Enter crackers. Apparently, crackers are like X-boxes for toddlers. I suppose that somewhere, sometime, there was a kid who actually ate a cracker in a restaurant. But I've never seen it. Somehow, what starts as a form of teething on the cracker turns to banging and breaking until increasingly smaller bits are formed. This activity somehow escalates into a primitive form of nuclear fusion, which scatters the cracker fallout in an estimated fifteen-foot radius, leaving nothing in its path unpolluted. Cracker people are oblivious to the fallout. The rest of us, however, are not, as it generally takes a CERCLA superfund crew a day to restore the affected area. One thing, though. Cracker people tip well. If they tip well, you can put up with a lot more.

Which leads us to drinkers. As a category, drinkers are the most enjoyable group. They are not usually in a hurry, spend more money than any other group, and usually tip accordingly. Note, I said usually. *Exception: There's a slight danger of drinkers becoming ten feet tall and bullet-proof. In which case they are not so fun to deal with.*

The crowd starts to arrive and you're section gets sat. A group of four suits. This keeps the door on your theory open just a little longer. You approach the table with the new girl in tow. You make the introductions and take a drink order. On the way back to the wait station to log the order, you explain, *Suits are the tables you want. They tend to come equipped with expense accounts and they're not afraid to use them.*

≡

As the crowd thins and things start to slow down, you ask, *Any questions you can think of?*

I'm sure there will be lots as I try to get the hang of this. But for now, I just want to know what you call people who don't fall into one of your categories.

It is as if the heavens have opened up and a great light has shone down upon you and your prodigy. Whatever you thought or felt about her before, you might have just fallen in love. You stand beaming for a few seconds and look up at me as if to capture all the glory you can in this moment by rubbing it in my face. Without missing another beat, though, you answer.

Samantha's first training session at *café rembrandt* is coming to a close. Which is good, because you are starting to run out of material. So you ask again if she has any questions.

Just one thing. Jillian called you Hemingway. What's that about?

Oh that. It's because I'm also a writer. You confess, somewhat sheepishly.

Really? What have you written?

I have to turn away from the bar to keep from laughing out loud. As much as I'd love to hear you wiggle out of this, I don't think I can control myself, so I pick up a rack of dirty glasses and head to the kitchen.

⚍

As soon as the lunch crowd is gone and what is left of the staff is busy doing checkouts and rolling silverware I retrieve your notebook. I didn't dare pick it up before the shift. For one thing, if it was bad, I didn't want to have to answer questions. I don't know what I was expecting to find, but I am surprised by what is there:

Purple flowers on a young tree east of the house. Reaching up with long gangly arms over the fence. Dropping petals in the yard as spring goes about its fickle way. Rushing forward, loafing, and turning back.

I am at once happy and sad. The realization of simple beauty is almost too much to take. I have to turn away.

I want to take all the emotion inside me and pour it onto the page. To get rid of it. To stop its taunting riddles. It speaks a language I don't understand. I want to see its face, know its name. Just there, beyond my reach lies my genius. Hiding in plain sight behind the sheer curtains of uncertainty.

If I can't have this one thing, then I want nothing. It's not too much to ask. And yet, I know it's everything.

LOVE: STUDY 3

love tells dirty jokes.
love makes you laugh.
love goes down on you.

love comes right away.
love can go all night.
love is a thief.

love gives it away.
love pours your bath.
love doesn't bathe.
love cooks for you.
love eats your food.
love borrows your car.

love drives too fast.
love fucks you in the front seat.
love brings you wine.

love opens your best bottle.
love gazes at stars.

love reads poetry.
love sleeps past noon.
love forgets to pay its bills.
love wears wrinkled linen.

love ignores the laundry.
love forgets to eat.
love wanders

out the door
without shoes.
love jaywalks.

DILLON

I pour a shot of whiskey and consider what I am about to say. It isn't the sort of thought I'd reveal to most people. But two things persuade me. One, that you aren't most people. And two, it occurs to me it isn't my choice to make. The words have already spilled into my head ready-made to be spoken and it isn't my job to censor them.

Even though your relationship with the literature student was short-lived, you remain bereft. You've shown up on my doorstep on a Sunday morning, looking like you're as short on sleep as you are on perspective. Luckily, I've been up for a while reading the paper on my deck, so I've had some coffee already. You catch me in the middle of stirring up some fresh cream for my breakfast.

The whiskey is for your coffee. A friend used to say, while pouring brandy into his coffee, *What's the point of being awake if you have no courage.* I walk out to the deck and hand you the cup. I am still working on *The Week in Review*, but push the other sections of the *Times* closer to you and tell you to help yourself. "I'm making some French toast, want some?"

Sure, you shrug as you plant yourself in a shaded seat. Heaven forbid you soak up a little sunshine.

I rinse some fresh blueberries to go with the cream and finish up the toast. When I return to the deck, you have inched your way into the sun. It is still spring and the mornings are chilly in the shade.

I serve breakfast and top off the coffee. I fold the paper next to my plate, thinking I'll let you make the first move on the conversation board. But other than commenting on the breakfast, you are silent. I start rethinking my decision. As you pick through your food, I pick through my words.

I am about to speak when you preempt. *Why do you think this happened?* Looking up from your plate finally. *Was I not paying attention? Not being grateful? Does this help me be a better person, somehow?*

I really have no idea where Dillon has gone. The real you is never so literal. The real you wouldn't ask me how I thought he could be a better person. I offer the best I can conjure up at the moment. *You know I don't believe in punishment. I don't believe there is some higher being that metes it out. That's just a cop out for situations we don't understand.* It is easy to fall back on religious conditioning and the idea that the gods are trying to punish you somehow. Easy for most people. But I can't help but feel you've been replaced by a twelve-year old version of yourself. One raised by religious parents, who still believes a loving God could condemn his children to a mythical Hell for a whole range of acts, including improper thoughts.

I decide not to skirt the matter any longer. *How many conversations have we had about synchronicity, about how things are mysteriously connected? About how you and I communicate with each other when we're not trying so desperately to put things into words?*

Like and unlike Phillip, you and I have both flirted with writing. We keep journals and even exchange poems from time to time. I've even submitted a few of mine for publication. But neither of us has had any illusion about becoming a professional writer. It's more about wanting to understand the thoughts in our heads and to see if we can recreate them on paper. Besides, who makes a living writing poetry anyway?

Like many things between us, poetry has become a kind of contest to see who can do it better. You've never paid much attention to the things you were supposed to learn for school, but you've always excelled at random and often obscure knowledge of history, literature, and music. Over the span of our friendship each of these categories has been fair game.

As for concepts like synchronicity, you are more cynical than me, but generally open to the idea that we can't explain how the universe works. Or how things are connected, just that they are. Today though, I'm trying to push you into deeper waters. And you are looking for a life jacket.

Are you saying that I communicated with her telepathically? Come on. I think that's something I would remember. Even if, what has that got to do with anything? You are stubbornly trapped in an unfamiliar world of straight lines and nicely wrapped packages. Grade-school safe explanations and dictionary entries.

I'm saying more than that. I'm saying you may have facilitated the whole thing. On an invisible plane, it's possible you coordinated their meeting. I say, unflinchingly. We are not in the business of coddling one another. And, miserable as you may be over the dumping, I see no reason to break out the kid gloves.

You stop staring at your plate and shift your focus in my direction as my words knock at the door of your heart. I scoot my chair back and pick up our plates, leaving you to consider this riddle on your own for a minute. While I'm inside, I grab the coffee pot and the bottle of whiskey.

When I return to the table again, you seem more focused.

Okay, let's say for a minute you are right, and that this is possible, and that it is, in fact, what happened. Why would I want to do such a stupid thing? The whiskey might finally be working, as this is the smartest thing you've said in days.

I think you have to step outside your grief for a minute to answer that. You have to consider the possible mutual benefits. What did she need and what did you need that you neither one felt comfortable asking for out loud. I'm not sure I can answer that question. But I'm pretty sure if you could bring Dillon back for a couple of minutes, he could.

You finally crack a smile. *I think it's pretty fucking obvious what she got out of it. But I don't see any benefit of the bargain here for me.*

Okay. If I must break out the spoon and start to feed you, what about this: She made you feel alive again in ways you thought were dead. Remember how you told me you wanted to be in love again. Really, madly, crazy in love. How much you missed the electricity and spontaneity that used to come with making a new connection. Well. She did that. And don't try to tell me it's not true. Why do you think you're so fucked up over this one? You've been, what's the word, quickened.

You consider this at some length. *Let's consider that what you're saying—loony as it may be—is true. That all things in life are connected. That much of what happens to us is played out on some invisible plane. That I have in fact been quickened by some silent agreement I made with her. What do I do with this?*

Let's see, you've had you heart broken, are experiencing profound self-doubt, are considering again the idea that perhaps all things in life are invisibly connected, and now you're left totally without direction or purpose. What is the only responsible thing left to do?

Get drunk? You ask.

Okay, fair, but after that?

I give up.

Here's a hint: Time to pack the backpack and find your passport.

TWO PARTS

THE PAINTER

The painter stood at the top of the crude staircase, temporarily eclipsing the frail light that struggled up from below the street. Beyond his shadow, the pale glow that escaped the cellar caught its reflection in the luminescent honeycomb shaped puddles of the cobbled street that still shimmered with the memory of the painter's shoes.

The painter was not one to leave his house unnecessarily. He had, as you know, a singular focus, often staying in his studio for days at a time. But his route was not direct, was not that of a man driven by a singular purpose. Instead, the route he invented as he made his way included a wander around the Quarter. Along the way, he managed several distractions. Including a pub where he enjoyed a stein of beer and a conversation with a local miller before he departed for the street again.

Color was hard to come by in his country. He allowed himself these walks because in this neighborhood he could gather a little color, which was as essential to him as air.

In the cellar lived a gallery. Run by a merchant who was neither dishonest nor entirely honest, but who would greet the painter with open arms. The merchant was reputable.

Not necessarily for being fair, but because he had a way of getting his hands on important pieces. Pieces for which he knew the painter would pay too much. He knew the painter was not capable of concern over money.

The painter descended the staircase and stood for a moment in the doorway before pushing open the door. Having gathered some color, he was now in search of light.

MAGGIE

You sit across the table from her. She wears an unstructured cotton dress stamped with a pattern of yellow flowers worn thin with too many washings. What the generation before you would call a housedress. Her hair is unwashed. Her nails chewed down and straight across. You anticipated this. You did not wear a suit, but blue jeans with a cotton blouse and a simple khaki blazer. You wanted to be professional. But not intimidating.

She did not offer you coffee. Or even a Diet Coke. She opened the door with a cigarette in her hand. She continues to smoke and to flick the ashes incessantly into a melted plastic ashtray, turquoise with deep brown staccato cigarette burns. Stains almost the same shade as the rusted legs on the kitchen table.

Awkward does not approach what you feel. There may not be a word yet for what you feel. Death does different things to different people. It has immobilized her. She has lost all forward motion.

I suppose what I want to know is whether there is anything I can do for you. You finally manage.

No. The reason you are here is because of what I can do for you, right? Her response is fired back without flinch or hesitation. Her gaze is as straight and direct as her words.

It isn't going like you hoped. Not that you thought it would be easy. She lost her only son. More than ten years ago. Not that she knew who he really was. She didn't know about the drugs or the graft. She didn't know about the violence. Nor will you tell her these things. Because if thinking he died honorably has left her in this state, imagine what the truth would do to her. Can you take anything from an empty shell?

You realize that while you know almost nothing about her, she knows exactly who you are. You are not the first person to come here looking to purchase her mercy, to trade it for sympathy, for sad stories about the human condition. She will not barter. You have nothing she wants.

While you were still in law school, she was talking to investigators, being coached by seasoned prosecutors. Her grief was still fresh. She may have even believed then that there would be a day when it would fade, become like the wallpaper, like the pattern on her dress. Now though she has lived this story for ten years. And her grief is the only thing left of her. Tucked safely inside her shell of quiet rage. The whole package nearly invisible. If you saw her at the grocery store, you wouldn't remember her.

Of course, you are here because her sworn statement of mercy wouldn't hurt your client. Fighting the death penalty requires you to use every tool in the shed. And forgiveness is often the sharpest one. More useful than mitigation. More persuasive than any legal brief. But you also want to know. You need to do more than imagine what it is to be her. You have to sit here in her house, breathing her air, suffocated by the heavy layers of pity. You have to feel her inexplicable guilt at outliving her son. And her rage. Her palpable rage at your client, at you, at her now ex-husband who crumpled under the weight of this, even at her son. At a world that has used her up, a god who has abandoned her.

You had to know these things. But you did not know what it would be like. You could not have guessed it would feel like this. You are afraid to speak, because each wrong word will lead you closer to the door. Suddenly you have no idea why she agreed to meet you.

Both your hands are folded on top of the file in your lap. She occasionally uses both of hers to light one cigarette off another. The rest of the time one hand holds—and taps—the cigarette while the other gets tangled in her dirty hair. The file contains a number of things you thought, before coming here, might possibly interest her. Mercado's prison record, a series of letters he has written to her but never mailed, his artwork, and a draft of your Petition. You can't imagine now how any of this will matter.

I'm here because I'm trying to stop another killing from taking place. And yes, I intend on asking you to help me. And I understand how unlikely it is that you will agree to do that. You pause only briefly to consider the contents of the file. Then, continuing to return her direct gaze, you remove the elastic band and reach inside the file, retrieving a single sheet of paper. As you place it on the table in front of her, you explain, *Steve wanted me to give you this. He instructed me not to make any copies of it or use it in his appeal in any way. You may read it or throw it in the trash. But I hope you give it some thought before you do either.*

 The letter consisted of three short paragraphs. It was the first one Mercado had written to her:

> *If you had been the cause of my son's death, I'm not sure I could manage to forgive you, ever. So I understand and respect your desire that my death sentence be carried out. I am not writing to beg for your mercy.*

> *I am writing because I played a role in taking something from you, something I can never return or pay back. I want you to know that I am sorry for what happened that night. I am sorry that you are suffering. And I regret that there is absolutely nothing I can do to ease that suffering.*

Someday I may get the courage to explain to you what happened that night. But I will only do it if I can convince myself it will do you more good than harm to know the truth. I am not a religious man. But if there is a God, I hope that he blesses you and gives you some measure of comfort.

Sincerely,

Steve Mercado, #091101

She does not look at the letter on the table. Instead, she continues looking at you, through the thin line of cigarette smoke marching single file towards the ceiling to join the gathering there. Yet, you detect something, a slight shift, a nearly imperceptible retreat of intensity. For the moment, it is enough. Enough to keep you there a little longer.

JILLIAN

Had I walked here
I could tell you stories
of how the uneven cobblestones
tugged at the souls of my feet
(with their promises of old men's tales,
the linger of pipe smoke)
or how water gathered between them
when it rained;
and how that rain opened
my senses,
the palms of blossoms,
the possibilities of flowers;
how these things lured
stirring wanderlust,
pulling me deeper
through narrow corridors
past bright colors
down paths dimly lit
by lamps of faded
(you thought I'd say)
memory

is an illusion
a rain barrel overflows,
petals fall loose
and I am soaked
with longing to revisit
places I've never been,
but remember.

DILLON

You touch down in Hamburg. Spend a week with friends in a little college town nearby. You learn how to read the train schedules and to navigate through a restaurant menu. You pedal a rusted cruiser. You name cities to conquer. You board a train and set out on your own. You write to me from Berlin.

You've only been there two days and already you've met a girl, claimed a local bar, and befriended an old artist who has become your tour-guide.

The girl thing happened like this.

While bar-hopping in Berlin and cruising through the listings in your guide book, a bartender suggests an opera. *La Bohème.* I can tell you first hand that's an odd suggestion from a bartender, so something in your conversation must have led to that. Three things happen in opera: people suffer, people are temporarily happy, and then people die, sometimes in rapid succession. I don't know if you confessed to the bartender that you hold season tickets to the opera here at home. In the States, most bartenders would probably be reluctant to offer this as an option for a single male. But in Europe, the opera is a little more sexually ubiquitous. You look it up on your map and note the time.

During intermission at the opera, you keep your eyes on a young Prussian girl with café au lait skin as you make your way to the bar to get two glasses of something red. There doesn't appear to be anyone with her, so you walk up to her casually. You try out your best book-read German while introducing yourself and offering her the wine. (I'm sure this is not a pretty sight—and I would love to be there so I could tease you mercilessly.) As if the awkward-American-unilingual-boy display isn't enough, just as you approach, her girlfriend returns from the restroom. There is an unmistakable moment of awkwardness where all three of you know exactly what the trouble is but have no idea what to do about it. Just in time though, the patron saint of pick-up moves whispers in your ear and you hand your untouched glass of wine to her friend and excuse yourself to fetch another. An objective reporter might take this as the first sign that you've left your heartbreak on the other side of the pond, but I'm reserving judgment.

When you return again from the bar, you continue to muddle through some less-than-conversational phrases that bear some semblance to the German language. Fortunately, the Prussian Cinderella puts an end to the torture by placing her fingers to your lips. She politely explains that English was a required course in school for years. Recognizing your singular language situation, the two girls decide to let you down off your linguistic cross and begin to ask you questions in English. Eventually, the flush disappears from your face and you start explaining what you've seen in Berlin so far. Soon the lights blink in the lobby and the girl—Sofia—takes your hand and leads you back into the theatre where there just happens to be an extra seat beside theirs.

After the performance, you invite them both to dinner. You all hop a train to a little trattoria in their neighborhood. The waiters know the girls and dote over the three of you all night. Though young, the girls are both well-read and well-traveled by American standards. At the end of the meal, the waiter brings a round of liquor to the table. He whispers to you that it is on the house as he lights the liquid inside the tiny glasses.

After dinner, the girls walk you back to the train. Your bag is still at a train station on the other side of Berlin and you aren't sure where you're going to sleep. Sofia suggests a backpacker-friendly spot that is directly on the bus line from there. It's a little distance from the café district, but charming.

While walking down *Schlesische Strausse* in the dark, coat buttoned up against the wind, wool scarf around your neck, you approach the hostel. Beside it, the street front windows of *café Eins* peer out into the night. The lights are still on, but the crowd is sparse. Of course, you've already had plenty to drink, but you don't feel the night is quite ready for bed. It's still tugging at your shirt, wanting you to come play. You feel the comfortable warmth on your face as you pull open the door to the café.

One of the few late-nighters is an old man sitting at the bar. You pull your shoulder pack over your head and take a seat next to him. Encouraged by your ease at making friends so far, you ask what he is drinking. Language barriers and apparently a generous number of *biers* stand in the way of his answer. The bartender lends an interpretation. The old guy insists on buying the bier.

He apologizes several times for his broken English and each time you assure him the apology is completely absurd, you being in his country and all. Despite the language barrier, with some effort you both manage to carry on what passes for lively conversation into the (even more) wee hours.

He's lived in Berlin since long before the wall came down. You ask about the changes in East Berlin. He answers that history has been essentially erased. The line for a while, he says, was that East Berlin was the biggest construction site in the world. Almost all the old structures were torn down. Buildings, monuments, parks. He said that had been the fate of the city throughout history. Whenever a new regime took over, the city was overhauled to pay homage to the new power. Berlin is beautiful, even in the cold of spring, but something eerie remains. The government could remove the old statues, build new shiny buildings, but couldn't exorcise the sad spirits of the past.

Despite these things, the old man seems to possess an unshakable happiness, an entitlement to its proceeds. After all, he makes his living as a painter. He spills out his emotion on canvas, acknowledges it, expresses it, moves on. And even gets paid to do it. Your conversation with him reflects your mutual joy: yours for being free in the moment, traveling, exploring, meeting new and interesting people; the old painter's for having had the good fortune of a life lived on his own terms.

Your new friend asks you how long you are staying in Berlin. You tell him you're leaving in a few days for Prague. Then Vienna; then Munich. Then back to San Francisco. But when you mention Vienna, his lights turn on. He tells you that *Wien* is his favorite place in the world.

Your travel notebook is sitting on the bar, and the old guy gestures for it. You turn to a blank page and hand it to him, along with a pen. The painter writes four things. As near as you can decipher, they are: Bauernmarkt (underlined twice); Belverdere: Gust Klimt; Stephen Dom: (with an arrow to) Cellar; and Fieglmuller (with an arrow to) Wienerschnitzel (underlined four times). He tells you to try to take a daylight train into Vienna, as the mountains on the way are not to be missed.

After a while, the painter decides it's time to go home, while he can still take advantage of the blanket of night for sleep. You agree to meet back the next night and report on your day in Berlin. You thank him for his suggestions, and he makes an exit. Following an old habit, you stay and talk with the bartender while she closes down. And that is how you find your bar.

The next day you awake with a bittersweet pain in your head. Ordinarily, you would have gone back to sleep for a while, but hangovers are more tolerable when you're on holiday. You roll out of bed, pull on some boxers, grab your room key and shower bag, and walk carefully down the unnecessarily dark hallway. Your hangover is thankful for the darkness, but your feet are having trouble remembering their way without some assistance. Just as you turn the first corner in the hall, you trigger a sensor and a light comes on as you pass under it. You laugh, thinking about the secret superpower you've had since childhood to turn on and off streetlights as you pass under them. It must work in Europe, too.

After you dress, you re-pack your shoulder pack, careful to include anything you might need for the day: books, journal, camera, maps, pens, money, condoms (an optimistic move). Then you make your way down the stairs to the desk, lights blinking on as you reach each new flight. You pick up some pamphlets at the front desk and walk through a curtain towards the exit.

The warm smell of fresh baked bread greets you as you open the door again to café Eins. You pull your shoulder pack off over your head and take a seat at the bar. Funny how a place changes between night and day. The same view from the same barstool is virtually unrecognizable from the night before. Somewhere around noon the metamorphosis begins. As the world changes its pace, the hum of conversation is different. The light changes. The mood changes. The people are different.

Why is it that the same place is more comfortable at different times in the day? There are questions like this we ask ourselves all the time. They seem fundamental to our lives, to who we are. But months or years may go by before you think about them again. They usually come back, like an old friend or a book you misplace and find years later. Even though it feels like you own the thought, like it is yours to file away and keep, the truth is that someday you will have the thought for the last time. Maybe it gets caught in some cosmic eddy and never makes its way back to you. Feeling a sudden sense of urgency to capture it before it disappears again, possibly forever, you quickly write down the question in your journal.

Your breakfast, known here as *frühstück,* includes three kinds of fresh breads, fresh fruit, musli with cream and honey, and orange juice. Plenty of nourishment to soak up last night's fun. Oh yes, and coffee, rich, dark, wonderful coffee with steamed milk, known here as *milchkaffee.*

You eat and drink with the luxury of someone who has no place to be, no marching orders to follow. You pull out your travel journal during the meal and glance at the suggestions the old painter wrote for you. One of the hardest things about travel is the struggle between *being* and *doing*. There will be plenty to see and do, and you won't see or do all of it. But if you'll just remember you are on vacation, it probably won't matter as much. Trying to pay homage to this simple but paradoxical rule, you order more milchkaffee and linger for as long as you can possibly sit still.

When adventure finally will have no more of this, you fold up the napkin from the café and place it inside your journal along with the bookmark from Die Fabrik, the various U-Bahn maps, museum guides, receipts, and other scraps of paper which will later act as guide ropes, Ariadne threads to lead you back here. You put these things into your shoulder bag, a trustworthy companion over the years which has played Sherpa to everything from the words of poets purchased at City Lights to left-over étouffée in the Big Easy. Now it is being rewarded with a trip to Europe. Mimicking a motion you've repeated thousands of times, you lift the shoulder strap over your head and a few steps later you begin a nostalgic walk up *Schlesische Strausse* to the haupft bahnhauft.

WORDS: STUDY 3

words are demanding lovers.
you must take your time.
turn down the lights,

gather the candles, put on music.
you must remember poetry
and forget expectations.
you must speak of their beauty
and swoon at their voices.
you must stand naked before them

and allow them their mystery.
you must ask them to talk
and then remain silent.

PHILLIP

From my post I watch you continue your training of Samantha. If that's what it can be called. It is more like an extended episode of one of those brain-numbing dating shows. It would be funny if it weren't so pathetic. I wonder if you have any idea how transparent you are. Or if you care. I wonder if Virgil knew what he was doing when he left the task to you.

You walk up to the bar while I'm cutting limes and pull a napkin off the stack. You take a pen from your apron and scribble out four letters. Then you turn back to Samantha to continue your laboriously intricate game of cat wants to get in mouse's pants.

Not everything makes sense in this restaurant world. *For instance, did you know,* you say as you hand her the napkin with the letters G-H-O-T spelled out on it, *that this spells fish?*

Looks like göt to me. Samantha swiftly replies. For a prey animal, she seems far too unaware of her surroundings. I'm not sure she is quick enough to stay ahead of even the dopiest cheetah. Fortunately, that is all she has to contend with here.

Nooo. Oh, I'm sorry, our challenger falters. But don't worry, the English language is a mysterious and slippery thing. Let me show you why: 'gh' is pronounced 'f' as in enough. The 'o' is pronounced as an 'i' as in women. And the 't' is pronounced 'sh' as in vacation, temptation, revelation, and fornication."

Or, masturbation. I know it's an obvious addition, but I can't help but interrupt your little charade.

You turn your head to acknowledge the slight, but say nothing and then quietly turn back to her, as if to indicate that my sophomoric meddling was unworthy of comment. *Similarly, in the restaurant world, the language can be tricky. For instance, here, the word* with *actually means glass.* You pause, but not long enough for her to answer. *Why, you ask?*

Because we all skipped English class? I answer. Still trying to throw you off your game.

Well, not all of us. You retort.

Just those of us in charge of training today? I'm playing, well mostly, but I'm not sure your trainee gets it, so I throw in a wink.

No help from the studio audience, please. Comes your attempt to wriggle free. *The answer is that* with *is simply short for* with *a glass. Because not everybody drinks their beer out of the bottle. Execution: 'I need a Modelo, with.'*

⸻

You have a lot of clever banter at your command. You quote poetic and literary sources, but you miss the point. You so desperately want to be a wordsmith that you've overlooked the essential thing which would take you there. To put it in literary terms, you have made this girl a footnote when she ought to be in the title. And for all your talk of writers, books, and romance you have failed to study the one thing that matters: your subject.

After you've closed out for the day and your crimson tipped shadow has left the building, you sit at the bar for an after-shifter with your lanky arms draped out in front of you. Your posture is so chronically bad I sometimes wonder if you have a complete skeleton. I'm working a split shift that has blurred into a straight. While I restock from a busier than expected lunch rush, I listen to you make small talk. Eventually this includes a complaint that I'm jeopardizing your chances to get laid.

With more than a hint of disbelief in my voice, I answer, *Look, generally I'm in favor of people having sex. The world would be a better, more relaxed place if more people had more sex more of the time. But trust me when I say that my sarcastic interference is not your problem. If you can't clear the tiny hurdles I scatter in your path, how do you expect to perform when it matters?*

Ouch. Be nice. You wince, physically pulling away from my direction. I know your ego is more fragile than you let on, but I think it's important for someone to shake you up a bit. You use your charm and wit like grease to slip through life without noticeable difficulty or complication. Sometimes it's my job to hold up mirrors, sometimes it's to spray the runway, and sometimes it's to be the speed bump.

Why? I smile.

Because I'm just trying to make the world a better place? One pretty girl at a time. You feign a sheepish posture, but can't hold on to it, grinning shamelessly. I'm less put off by this than I pretend. But I continue restocking the bar and act like I'm unimpressed.

Ok, quick question for clarification: What is your goal here? Part of me wishes I would have thought of a more clever way to ask the question, but then we'd just be caught up in word games, which isn't the point.

You look at me blankly for a few seconds after I ask this. *I didn't know there was going to be a test, I swear. Nobody said anything about a test. I would have studied. I wouldn't have stayed out so late.*

It's not a trick question. Perhaps I act a little too annoyed when I say this.

Help me out here, Jillian. I didn't read the latest Cosmo. I'm not sure what I'm supposed to care about this week. What level of sensitivity do I need to display? Enough to anticipate your needs, while not coming off as spineless?

If this line were delivered in honest frustration, it would have been more effective, passionate even, but it came out so polished I know you rehearsed it. *Okay, I'll feed it to you. You want to write, don't you? Isn't that what you've been telling everyone since you were old enough to hold a pencil? Isn't that what all this literary posturing and wooing with Whitman is about?*

For an instant you look truly wounded and I almost back off. But I know your powers of recuperation are quick. So, before you regain your composure, I strike with the final blow. *Here's what I see. You will never write a single thing that is worth reading until you start to figure her out.*

Her? You point at a door she walked through nearly an hour ago. *Why her? Why is she special? You don't even like her. Do you?*

That isn't the point.

You cover your face with one hand, your eyes peering through your fingers. You appear to actually be thinking about this for a few seconds. You open your mouth once as if to speak, then reconsider. A few seconds later, you try again, *The sexes have been trying—mostly unsuccessfully—to figure each other out since the beginning of time, and in the meantime a few people have managed to write a few things worth reading.*

The point is for you to want *to figure her out.* I toss down the bar towel and lean in towards you. *She is your subject, and you should be panting to get into her head, not just her bed. A fuck is just that. And unless you're planning on writing porn, it isn't very interesting to read about. What people think when they're not fucking, that's interesting. I've had lots of conversations that were more erotic and more intimate than most sex.*

With this, I walk around the corner of the bar, untie my apron and trail it over the back of a barstool. Then I slide up next to you and stand uncomfortably close. I lean towards your ear, bending almost enough to give you a glimpse of my bare breasts beneath my shirt. But not quite. I curve one hand around the back of your neck and—almost touching your ear with my lips—I whisper, *Anticipation. Longing. Unfulfilled desire. That is the human condition.* Then I turn my face to the right, my open mouth closing in on yours, and I lean in so close you can feel my breath as it softly quickens its pace. I feel your eyes close. I wait. Hovering there for almost too long. Counting the beat of your pulse. And gently I retreat, running my hand from behind your ear, down your neck and along your chest as I slowly walk away.

LOVE: STUDY 4

love eats chocolate.
love dips you in peanut butter.
love melts in your hands.

love gets on your sheets.
love opens your best wine.
love wears your favorite sweater.

love takes off your clothes.
love lives under your skin.
love stains your heart.

MAGGIE

*J*ill? You ask, as if my name alone were a complete question.

I look up from the three-sink where I'm washing glasses. I hesitate, waiting for more, until I think maybe that's it. *Yes, love?* I finally answer.

I like the wrong people. Sometimes on purpose. Why do you suppose that is?

Your words spell out a question, but your intonation says something else. *Hmm. I get the feeling there is more to that statement.* I bait, wiping my hands on a bar towel.

I like the wrong people. I know it. I can see it pretty much from the beginning and I can't help myself. You reach for a menu, even though you know it by heart.

Love, we all like people who are wrong for us sometimes. I consider the lineup and hold up a batch of grapes. You shake it off. Along with a second choice. You continue to talk, as I offer up a veteran goose. You nod and I fill a shaker with ice.

What I mean is there are things about men that are deal-breakers for me. Their hands for instance. Or their voice. Or they have a worldview too incompatible with mine. But there will be something else there that makes me get involved with them anyway. A striking pair of eyes. Or a certain kind of charm. I don't mean players. They could be computer geeks. But something about them holds my interest. And I can't walk away. You keep fumbling with the menu, turning the pages back and forth.

Maybe I'm not following you, but it doesn't sound so far like you're describing the kind of wrong person I had in mind. I was thinking more along the lines of the unemployed, unbathed, hot-tempered, charming-as-hell-anyway, bad-boy types. I do know what it means to be with someone you shouldn't, no matter the type. I have crossed that line. And re-crossed it. I have seduced them and I have let myself be seduced. I have been reckless, knowing it will not end well. But knowing that makes it even more irresistible.

Aren't those little things also what makes us love someone, their quirkiness? I offer. I mean, I want my lovers to have something interesting and unique about them, something I can't quite pin down. I nod to the menu to see if there's a reason you're still holding it.

I suppose, you begin, ignoring my prompt, *but what I'm talking about is that for me these things, these little external oddities, they stand for something bigger. Something inside them which is utterly incompatible with me. Something which will come to override whatever temporary fascination I have. I know I have no future with them. I know it isn't the right thing to do. I know that I am lying to myself. And to them. And I do it anyway.*

I think the difference between us is that you tend to get stuck in these little lies because you aren't honest about what you're doing. Perhaps you're really looking for something like permanence, but can't admit it. So you lie to yourself. And to your lovers. I don't have any interest in permanence, in forever. I am there strictly for pleasure, and to satiate caprice. I make no promises that this is a permanent gig.

I think you might need food. I finally say.

Yeah, you're probably right. If I get some pasta chips will you have some? You finally close the menu and set it down.

Sure. I enter the order and pour some ice in a stemmed glass. Followed by a splash from a green bottle and a stream of water.

I guess I'm wondering why you're focused on this piece of the story. Don't you think there are so many other things you both get from your time together? Why do we expect everything to be forever. When there's no guarantee of that whatsoever. I realize this is a bit beyond your question. We all have delusional or self-destructive stories we tell ourselves. It seems to come with being human. I pick up the shaker and force the two contents to get to know each other a little better.

I don't know. I guess it just seems like such a waste of time. I don't know what I get from it. Another human to hang out with for a while, maybe. To distract me from myself and my neurotic mind?

You wrinkle your nose and wait as if for me to affirm that this is a legitimate reason. I don't. Who am I to tell you.

Instead I pick up a tiny spear and run it through two pieces of green fruit. Then I toss the contents of the glass in the sink. I place the speared fruit in the wet glass and drizzle the frozen liquid over the top until the shaker is empty.

When you don't get a response from me, you start to flip through the pages of the menu again. *Well it seems that my pattern is to run from love when things start getting too entrenched. That I go through these cycles of connecting and then disconnecting. I've been doing it since I was 16, I think. But truthfully, I might be getting too old for it. It's a little exhausting.* You close the menu again and lay your head on top of it for a few seconds. Then you sit up again and run your hands over your face and through your hair. Again you look up at me as if to cue my next line.

Here's what I think. I think it's possible you use relationships as a place to hide from love. They are stopovers between longing and heartbreak. And I think you hide there, inside the house of a relationship, until restlessness starts playing her guitar on your front porch. Until that moment when you know you can't hide there anymore. You simply can't stay in bed a minute longer, you have to go outside and throw some coins in her hat.

I set the glass in front of you.

JILLIAN

Sometimes a chair looks
like a nice place to rest.
Or maybe just to lean back,
to see the world a little.
A wall could look like
almost anything.
Sometimes a face looks
like a nice place to see.
Maybe it is sometimes.
Or a wall in the hole
so the world can't see a little.
Sometimes the strangest of places
become small,
swallowed by something
that looks maybe like a wall.
Or not something else.
Sometimes the smallest of faces
become strange.
Swallowing somethings
you thought you knew a little.

Sometimes we build somethings
that don't look like walls.
But feel just as small,
because we can only see a little.
Sometimes someofus see something
slight, so we step outside.
Staying out of jail
Sometimes becomes a prison.
If somepeople knew
they could escape.
Doesn't it seem like they would?

DILLON

Your feet catch you as you jump off the train. Your eyes begin their descent down the cement stairs and into the bleak corridor leading to the station. It's after midnight. And it's obvious right away this is no longer Germany.

A rusted sign overhead displays red characters that resemble the Russian alphabet you studied in school. But you can't make out a word. For an instant, you think you're in a bad cold-war apocalyptic movie where the evil Russians have taken over the world. The alphabet is not Russian of course, but Czech. And this is not some post-apocalyptic scene, but merely a dirty Czech train station in the middle of the night. Still, to a first-time visitor it's unnerving.

Once inside the lighted station, you collect yourself and begin to survey your surroundings. On the train you read in the guidebook that there is a 24-hour visitor's center located in the station. You find it without much trouble, but there's one problem. Cleverly forsaking its namesake, it is closed.

About then, a friendly face approaches and asks if you need a room. Luckily for you both, you had also read that a common form of accommodation in Prague was the flats offered by locals. Otherwise you might think this guy was a scam artist or some kind of nut. (You'll soon find out he is a nut, but for different reasons.)

You accept, the price is agreed upon, and you and your new host set off for the flat. This takes *far* longer than it should. Although the flat is in walking distance from the station, for reasons not clear, the two of you stand for what seems like hours waiting for a bus, which connects with another bus, which drops you a short walk from an industrially plain stucco building about five stories high. He uses a key to enter the door at the bottom and you climb up several flights.

Once inside the flat, your temporary landlord goes to unnecessary lengths inventorying all the things in the flat. It's quite Spartan—in the modern sense of the word—so that is not an exaggeration. He actually inventories *all* the things in the flat; those things that you can use (not many) and those that are not for guest use (most of them). He recites both categories with the same dumb smile and enthusiasm.

He reiterates several times that this room is "just for you." You take this phrase to mean that the room and the rate are special, and that your host is offering the deal *just for you*. You consider it part of his strange sales pitch, probably given to all tired travelers nabbed in the middle of the night in the bleak train station.

Meanwhile, he repeats all instructions at least a half dozen times: *here is a nice chair* (he brags); and *here is a bed you may sleep in* (although there are no sheets, only a paper-thin, scratchy, polyester bedspread); *there are no towels for guests* (but you are welcome to use this oversized napkin); *please don't use any of the shampoo, conditioner or soap* (as these are not covered by the rent); *you may use this tiny transistor radio* (but don't play any records on the turntable, you might scratch them); *the kitchen is not for you.*

He rambles on: *here is your key* (you can't help but think it is odd that a stranger is giving you a key to his flat); *here is a city map* (about the helpful size of a post-card) *oh yeah, I'll be wanting that back;* (and of course) *this room is just for you.* Slowly realized translation: Don't bring any prostitutes up here, because they are bad news, will probably steal something that even guests are not allowed to use, and then I'll have to deal with the police (that the police are to be avoided at all costs is universal).

There are other tedious instructions accompanying the inventory: how the lights inside the flat work, followed by several demonstrations; where the shoes go (on the rug by the front door); how the blinds open and close. All of these are repeated *ad nauseam* while your head spins with sleep deprivation. Still you attempt to listen carefully to each instruction as if it were going to be something new or important. Eventually you can stand no more. You find yourself nearly pushing him out of his own flat, so you can go to sleep.

⸺

By the next afternoon, you've wandered a bit, walked the streets, taken a bus tour, and now you are sitting in an upstairs café and listening to Frank Sinatra's Summer Wind while sipping a Pivo.

You've been walking everywhere today. Partly because you really want to see the city, to walk in the sun and to take in the architecture. And party because you still haven't figured out the public transportation system here. You don't understand the machines that distribute train tickets, and you can't read a word of Czech.

In contrast to your first impression, Prague is a beautiful city. The charm of its architecture and old world feel are hard to deny, though you have yet to fall in love with it. Something about it still seems tired. It isn't the dirt, you don't mind dirty cities: San Francisco, New York, New Orleans. Maybe the dirt is just older here. Of course, Berlin is all you have to compare it to in Europe, and many places would suffer by comparison.

⸺

After exploring for the rest of the afternoon and late into the evening, you stop in another sidewalk café in the Staromstské námestí (Old Town Square) and order a red wine. The square is considered the heart of the old city, and it's much more colorful than the neighborhood where you've been sleeping. Apparently, this was the city's main marketplace as far back as the eleventh century. All roads in Bohemia used to lead to this square, and merchants from all over Europe gathered here. Now, the whole square is closed to traffic. And here sits little you, right in the middle of it. The world is bigger than our ideas of it.

⹀

You catch an early dinner and head back to the flat to try to catch up on sleep. You find your way back to the building easily enough, following your visual clues. However, getting back into the room proves to be much trickier. You unlock the door to the lobby and begin to climb the stairs to the third floor. Upon turning the first corner in the stairwell, the light becomes noticeably dimmer. Around the corner to the second floor stairs, it is almost impossible to see, and you have to feel your way up and step very carefully. Around one more corner and it's pitch black. You start to question how many flights you've ascended, how many corners you've turned. You don't remember which way the doors face and have no idea how you would distinguish the keyhole to your temporary front door from that of one of your neighbors. For that matter, you aren't sure if you could find a keyhole in any door. You have no idea how many steps it is from the wall to the doors and you don't really want to leave the limited security of the wall to find out.

You finally find the courage to move, to venture off the wall. What follows is an eternity filled with the taking of small shuffle steps until your hands finally find the wall on the other side. As your hands move along the wall and over a stranger's front door (not that your host is not also a stranger), you feel something like a large button from which you immediately pull back, thinking it's a doorbell. You breathe nervously and imagine a scene where someone answers and finds you out there in the dark. How would you explain? The neighbor would wonder why you had the landlord's key. And of course, they would probably suspect foul play. For if you were a true renter, the owner of the flat most certainly would have shown you how to get back to the room. Surely they all knew how thorough a person he was.

You slide along the next wall and up another flight (you are almost sure this is the one). Your hands continue along the walls again. The landlord had shown you his brass nameplate beside the door to the flat, but it wasn't written in Braille. Not that Braille would do you any good either, come to think of it. Just then your hand hits another large button, but before you can pull back, it's too late. You cringe and wait for the sound, wait for a neighbor to spring forth with accusations and calls to the police.

What happens instead is beautiful. Simple, yet almost miraculous: A light comes on. And you find yourself staring across the hall at the brass nameplate of your room. Like one who falls on the ice but gets up before anyone notices, you casually walk across the hall, insert the key, turn the lock, and stroll inside the flat.

Tomorrow night you will see more of Prague, the Charles Bridge, the old castle across the river, the State Opera House. And this time you will fall for her. Because the true magic of Prague belongs to her nights. She puts on her diamonds and her best features are highlighted, like a lover in candlelight.

WORDS: STUDY 4

words get stuck
in your throat.
words hang on

to your tongue.
words are hard to swallow.
words can leave a bad taste.

words are sweet.
words are bitter.
words take a while to digest.

PHILLIP

I'm acutely aware of the passage of time. And yet, I'll piss it away.

That's an interesting way to start a conversation. I respond.

You are beyond disheveled. You look like you've been up all night.

Single or double? I warm up the espresso machine.

Ah yes, a little liquid Ritalin should do the trick. Better make it a deuce.

Sounds like maybe you could use a little more discipline. Just glue yourself to the chair and stare at the computer screen until you start writing something. I offer.

I mean, you're right, I could always write more. But it doesn't really matter what I do. If I write a sentence, I think I could have written a better sentence. If I develop a storyline, I'll second-guess it. For every minute that passes, I spend another minute thinking I could have spent that minute better. I walk around in a constant state of buyer's remorse.

Sounds more serious than I thought. And like maybe your old nemesis, time, is involved.

I think the clocks have all been doping. They never used to be this fast.

Second thought, maybe caffeine isn't what you need. I say, as I add the lemon twist to the saucer and set the espresso in front of you anyway.

At least if I'm wired I have a fighting chance.

We must be vigilant against the fog monsters. They prey whenever there's too much blood in our caffeine system.

The thing is, since I decided I am actually going to write this novel, and not just talk about it, I have no real free time. There is an anvil over my head everywhere I go. And a pervasive sense of guilt if I'm doing anything else. It's like being Catholic without any of the benefits of confession. I can't even dip into the communal wine. You squeeze the twist and run it around the edge of the little cup as you talk, adding three cubes of raw sugar.

I laugh in spite of myself. One of those spontaneous grade school-type snorts that comes out before you can check it.

Nice. Laugh at my misery. You pretend to be hurt, but you can't help but crack a smile. It's probably a little of both. You shake your head in disgust and raise the tiny cup to your mouth.

No. It isn't that. It's just that, it's nice to see you finally have a reason to act like a tortured artist.

You feign an injury to your heart, clutching it with your right hand while looking at me in disbelief. Speechless. I shrug and go about preparing my own double espresso. Then I reach into the freezer for the ice cream. I dip out a scoop and let it slide off the oversized spoon and into the rich black liquid, nearly spilling some of the precious elixir over the rim.

Breakfast. I explain in response to your stare that is exaggeratedly quizzical.

How do you stay so skinny? You accuse.

I raise a brow, then grab a smaller spoon.

Look, I continue, *it seems to me, Phillip, that all writers suffer self-doubt. Camus to Hemingway. You should take comfort in the fact that you're in good company.* I scoop up a spiked spoonful of melting cream.

Thanks. Hemingway shot himself in the head. You say, looking up at me while barely raising your head off the bar.

I'm wondering if maybe you're also wondering if all this effort will be wasted? Will you spend all your attention on this one girl and still go home alone at the end of the night? I lick the ice cream off my spoon. You pretend you're unaffected.

Yeah, there is that. And I know there's no guarantee. But I just wish there were a wink from the universe or something. Something to let me know I've got a shot. There is an honest hint of desperation in your voice. I think this may be as close to self-awareness as you've ever been.

Maybe writing is a little like believing in God. It may be a waste of time, but then again.

Are you saying heaven is a publishing contract?

I'm saying heaven is getting to take off that one girl's pants, even if it takes a while to get there. I lift the affogato to my lips again and tip up the cup a little too far, leaving a trace of espresso-milkshake. I run my tongue over my lip, to clean up the mess.

You're saying writing is like chasing women? You prop yourself up on your elbows, still pretending not to notice my antics.

Yeah, it's just a longer chase... and probably more masturbation.

Nice.

Well. I lean down to your level, raising my eyebrows at you like I'm expecting an answer.

Well, what? You implore, defensively.

If you're so concerned about time, stop wasting it here. Go home and write. Or better yet, take a nap. You look like shit. I finish off my breakfast and put the cup in the sink.

You pick yourself off the bar, slam the last of your spro, and reach into your pocket.

Tell you what, I got the coffee. I say, holding up my hand like a stop sign. *I'm taking odds against time.*

REMBRANDT: STUDY 2

the painter ate words.
the painter was not a chef.
the painter was not a master.
a master controls his estate,
his offspring, his unskilled labor.
a master uses a firm hand,

a whip, his large penis.
a master sleeps lightly,
where the painter snored.
the painter owned nothing,
borrowed everything.
the painter left the gate open,

the cupboards unhinged.
his horses ran wild,
scraps littered the floors.
the mop lay dry in the corner,
the gardens spilled over the walk.
always the words showed up on time.

MAGGIE

You pour yourself a fresh cup of coffee from the French press. You've been staring at the Rembrandt papers all morning long. You keep going over them, your research and your notes, wondering if somehow you're missing something.

You find yourself in an unexpected paradox. You studied Native American law in school and are excited to be doing work in that field. And you are happy to be able help out the café. But you never expected you would be on the other side of a Native American land rights case and feel good about it.

And the Sowha's new chairman is not being much help. It took him two days to return your phone calls. When you asked for a face-to-face with him, he reluctantly agreed. To try to put him at ease, you asked if you could buy him lunch at the café. In person, he was a little more understanding, but his position was still, "The U.S. Government does what it wants. We have always been at their mercy." You've given up the idea of trying to persuade him to fight along with you. All you want now is for him not to oppose your actions.

Your research has given you a few good leads and few contradictions. Essentially, there are three paths that diverge in these woods. The first is a direct route: the land is already Sowha. The Sowha inhabited the land for more generations than anyone knew. They were here when the first European landed on the other side of the continent. Then came the gold rush of the 1840s and mining settlements started seeping into the basin. The Sowha had always been able to abandon their campsites for six months of the year and return to them each spring. From season to season, other tribes respected this as Sowha territory. But the white newcomers didn't share these manners. The Sowha were a peaceful people and some acquiesced to the diggers taking up residence along their shores because they believed their presence was temporary. Others in the tribe were not so passive and on occasion there were violent clashes between them and the miners.

The story of the native people here does not have a happy ending. Fences and permanent structures eventually made it impossible for the Sowha to travel back and forth to the high country any longer, or to hunt and harvest as they once had. Within less than a quarter century, most were driven from their homeland and forced to find other ways to survive, including working for their successors.

The Sowha had not forgotten about the theft. They petitioned Washington D.C. to reclaim their land, and in 1874 an Executive Order was issued declaring a parcel on the west side of the lake as "Indian Country." The Order mandated that the land "be withdrawn from sale or other disposition and set apart for the use of the Sowha." The total area was about 250 acres and *café rembrandt* sits on part of that land today.

You can't lease something to someone that they already own. So if the 1874 Order was a valid land grant, then the new Executive Order is invalid. The real problem is that the café doesn't have the bankroll to fund a long drawn out fight against the U.S. Government. Especially if the tribe is not willing to offer any help.

The second path traverses the fact that compensation was paid the Sowha for the land in the 1950s. The Indian Claims Commission was created by an act of Congress in 1947 to address the sad fact that by the mid-twentieth century, the North American tribes had been all but driven into extinction. They had been cut off from their native lands and divested of nearly all their economic resources. Under the Act successful tribal claimants could be compensated by the federal government for their losses. In 1948 members of the Sowha tribe filed a claim under this Act. They sought compensation for the lands and resources taken by the encroachment.

In order to be compensated under the Act, the Sowha had to prove: 1) prior to encroachment, the tribe actually resided within a fixed geographic area, the acreage of which could be determined; 2) that the Sowha had been removed from such geographic area involuntarily; and 3) that the nature of the taking was such that a dollar value for compensation could be determined and awarded.

The only thing that was certain was that the Sowha did not abandon this land voluntarily. Beyond that, there were several problems. First, the Sowha did not reside in this area as their permanent residence. Next, the Sowha could not delineate, with legal specificity, a fixed geographic area which was previously "theirs." And finally it was realistically impossible to compensate the Sowha with money for destroying the only way of life they had ever known. In the blink of an eye several millennia of their existence was ground to a halt.

Nonetheless, despite these questions, a settlement was eventually reached. The Sowha's asking price was $44 million. This number considered what 10,000 acres near the lake—along with the minerals and timber since removed—would have been worth in 1862. It was an honest request. And a modest one considering what had actually been taken from them. In 1958, the government paid $5 million to the tribe. At the time, that meant two thousand dollars for each member of the tribe, the remainder going into a tribal endowment.

The question still remains whether, in taking this money, the Sowha sold title to the meadow. There were a few Sowha who remained in the meadow. They constructed permanent housing and integrated into white culture, working as day laborers, cooks and gardeners. According to future complaints filed under the Indian Claims Act, all of which were dismissed, many of these Sowha did not opt to join the claim and did not accept any settlement monies. Was their title to the land extinguished as well?

There is a third path that could be taken. It meanders a little more than the first two. It begins with the fact that an Executive Order is not an Act of Congress, which is required to grant valid title to land. In 1871, Congress abandoned treaty-making with the American Indian tribes. After 1871, any grant of land, even if done by Executive Order, had to be ratified by Congress. It could be argued then that the recent Executive Order is not valid.

Even though the new Order creates a lease and not a land grant, it nonetheless grants certain title to the property, even if only for a limited time. Just as a renter holds a limited title to an apartment. If the recent Executive Order were rendered null and void, then things would return to the status quo, and the café could go on leasing from the tribe as before. It was unlikely that the Government would risk further political crises by attempting to take back the land from the tribe altogether.

There was even the possibility of trailblazing a fourth path. The café has an agreement with a sovereign nation. It is entitled to specific performance of that agreement without interference by the U.S. Government. The Government would be forced to acknowledge and honor the sovereignty of the tribe. But it would also be a direct hit on the Sowha, forcing them to uphold the contract with the café and forego the grant monies windfall. In short, the win/win needle you seek remains hidden.

DILLON

I know why you've come.
You want me to tell you stories

of dragons I have chased,
armor that men wear,

castles where we have dwelt.
But you must understand time.

Time begs
no forgivenesses,

gives no excuses,
won't be broken.

Though the mystics tell me
it bends.

So be time for me.
Just for a minute.

A s t r e t c h e d out second.
Remember the dream

of the blue speckled lizards
and find your place

in the dry river bed of time.
Don't try

to understand the movement
of water—it keeps its secrets

inside of stones.
Its poetry is there for you to read.

But only the lizards know why.
And something inside them

longs to breathe fire
into your settled soul.

DILLON

There is a planetary grid of high-energy spots around the globe, linked together in a mysterious pattern. Mystics pay visits to these spots to raise their consciousness. This electromagnetic web is said to have something to do with fault lines, volcanoes, and even ships disappearing into mysterious geographic triangles.

A number of natural and man-made wonders are at these points: The Great Pyramid of Giza, the ruins of Bimini (which some consider the lost city of Atlantis), the Amazonian Ruins, Stonehenge, the Ancient Cities of Peru, and Easter Island. Also on the grid are Lake Tahoe, Lake Baikal, the Galapagos Islands, and Rio de Janeiro.

⸺

Your train arrives in Vienna before sunset. A bi-level, bustling, modernized center, in complete contrast to the dark dungeon of the Prague station. You find the tourist center, exchange your Czech crowns for Austrian shillings and buy a pass for the train. You find a bank of phones and pull out your guidebook. You turn to the section for lodging and call a pension on the list. The price is almost twice what is listed in the guide, so you move to the next listing you circled. The clerk, a precise and articulate man, cites an acceptable rate, gives you directions by U-Bahn, and you set off for your lodging. Before you can get to the escalators, though, two young Americans approach you. They ask in English if you speak English. You think for an instant about pretending you are an Austrian native. But the backpack kind of gives you away. You nod, and they ask if you know of any places to stay. You motion for them to follow as you make your way back to the phones. You dial the pension again. They have an extra room, but only one. You arrange for a fold-out bed and reserve the room.

The U-Bahn takes the three of you into Central Vienna. The younger one introduces himself as Eric and his larger, slightly older companion says his name is Mark. They both thank you emphatically, but you shrug it off and say, *I'm just glad to find companions for dinner already. I'm Dillon.*

You emerge from the underground station onto another pedestrian plaza. Directly in front of you, the sky is partially eclipsed by a towering gothic cathedral, St. Stephen's. Also known as Stephensdom. Spiny spires that strain to touch the sky. Tiled rooftops. Overseeing gargoyles. You don't get a lot of this in America.

As the three of you make your way up Stephensplatz and through the center of town, the sun has just begun to fall beneath the horizon of the mountains in the distance. It reflects gracefully across the alabaster statues and brings out a sparkle on the widespread walkways of the Innere Stadt.

As you continue up the plush cafe and shopping district of Graben, you pass by five centuries of architectural style in St. Michael's Church. You turn left on Dorotheergasse to find the Pension Alcon, where you climb two flights of stairs until you come to a mezzanine with two unmarked doors. You try the buzzer at each door and eventually an unimposing man in his early thirties opens the south door. He is gracefully built, with close-cropped, dark hair. Distinguished, with just a touch of arrogance. He introduces himself as Stephan and ushers you all inside.

Stephan shows you your rooms and around the pension. He asks if the accommodations are satisfactory and then leads you to a tiny area tucked into the front of the main hallway, with a small counter, a phone, and a locked cabinet where keys and passports are kept. He collects your passports and shillings and hands out keys, explaining which ones unlock the downstairs doors and which ones are for the rooms. He then politely asks if there are any questions. Eric asks sheepishly if he can smoke in their room. To which Stephan replies, *You can smoke in your room, you can smoke in the breakfast room, you can smoke in the hallway, you can smoke in the toilet. Smoke wherever you want, this is not America.*

Once in your room, you set down your backpack, unfasten the top compartment and pull out your shoulder-pack. After a quick clean up in the bathroom down the hall, you pick up the shoulder pack and empty it of everything except a few pens, your journal, a thin book of poetry, and a camera.

You then descend a flight of stairs, turn a corner, and look in the doorway of the students' room to see if they are ready. Just lighting a cigarette, Eric welcomes you and offers his open pack.

Outside the pension, the sun has set. You turn to your companions and ask, *Which way?*

Mark and Eric shrug their shoulders. Eric says, *We've never been here.*

I know, but which way feels like the right way? You implore.

Blank looks. They turn to each other.

You stand still a minute until you catch the sensation. Left. *Let's go left.* The students follow.

Passing elegant boutiques, ice cafés, bakeries, chapels, and a few of Vienna's signature coffee houses, you decide on a small café. You are seated and order a bottle of red for the table. Your companions look panicked and explain they really can't afford it. *Neither can I,* you explain, *but I never let that stop me when I'm traveling.* This apparently does nothing to assuage their fear. *Relax. I've got it.* You assure. They seem okay with that solution.

For strangers from the same country who are brought together in a foreign land, the three of you find embarrassingly little to talk about. This is most disappointing to you, since you value conversation and connection over most things. You cover all the basics, where everyone is from, what university they are attending, what they're studying, how long they've been in Europe, what all they've seen, and when they are returning. But despite your efforts to drive it, the conversation lacks any life of its own. You try to talk books or movies or philosophy with them, but by the time dessert arrives, it is obvious this will be your last meal with these two. You didn't come all the way here to spend time with two Americans who are poor conversationalists. After dinner, they head back to their room to catch some sleep. Breathing a sigh of relief, you set out for more adventure.

The streets have thinned a little, with most people inside restaurants and cafés, eating, drinking, and telling stories. With fewer people around, you decide to break out your camera. You wander the plaza and its pedestrian side streets, capturing moments of light and time in fractured images. The St. Michael's Church, the nearby Loos Haus, the gateway to the Hofburg empire, the spire of the Rathaus, and then back to the figures lining the outside of the gateway.

After about an hour of tourist-immersion, you head down nearby Kärntner Strasse and duck into an art nouveau bar nearly a hundred years old. You talk with the bartender, who speaks fluent English because of his trade. A good way to get a feel for a place, to learn the locals' hangouts, the best places to eat, the best hours to see things, and countless other gems, is to talk to bartenders. The guidebooks can get you started, but let the locals take it from there.

You ask the bartender about where to eat and he mentions a vegetarian café on Bauernmarkt. *Whether you're vegetarian or not, it's not to be missed.* You make a note in your journal. When you finish your drink, you pick up your shoulder pack and pull open the century-old doors again. On the other side, you walk down Kärntner Strasse back towards your room at the Pension Alcon. Naturally, you allow yourself a distraction or two along the way.

The next afternoon, you head to the Belvedere museum, also recommended by the bartender. The Gustav Klimt work, *The Kiss*, is displayed there. You've seen the image on countless dorm walls and postcards, but you are not prepared for it in real life. It is so much larger than you imagined. The figures are life-sized, and the detail is so intricate. In contrast, the millions of reproductions have almost nothing to do with the actual piece. You stand in front of it for maybe twenty minutes, completely transfixed. As if Gustav himself were speaking to you through it.

While leaving the museum, you notice a young woman standing in front of another Klimt, sketching in a notepad. Despite your desire to find interesting people to talk to, you are sometimes quite shy, especially when it comes to meeting women. This time, you chicken out and carry on with your day's adventures.

You make your way down Bauernmarkt that evening to the vegetarian café, *Wrenkh,* suggested by the bartender the night before. You enter a glass door and step into a small entryway shrouded from the restaurant by long red velvet curtains. You consider your seating options and decide on a corner table against the back wall. As you walk over to seat yourself, you pass a young woman bent over a sketch pad accompanied only by a single beer in front of her on the table. Something about her is familiar, but you don't pay much attention. You remove your shoulder pack, turn, and slide into the corner table.

A man dressed in black soon shows up and speaks to you in German. You return a somewhat hopeless look and explain politely, *Ich verstehe nicht. Schuldigung, sprechen sie English?* He immediately switches to English and explains the evening's specials.

The wine comes, along with bread. You open Joseph Campbell's *The Power of Myth* and begin underlining passages, enjoying your food and small mouthfuls of wine. You read about the myth of Theseus and Ariadne. Theseus promises to love Ariadne forever if she can show him a way to make it into and out of the Labyrinth, so he can kill the Minotaur and not get lost forever. Ariadne gives him a simple ball of thread. He unwinds it on the way into the Labyrinth, slays the Minotaur, and then follows it back out. You wonder if the answers to life's hard questions can really be as simple as a ball of string.

When you finish the meal, you look up from the book to scan the café. You glance again at the woman to your left and then realize why she looks familiar. She is the woman from the gallery who was looking at the other Klimt. She is still busy sketching and is oblivious to your presence. The high point of your conversation in this city so far has been your host Stephan's instructions regarding smoking in the pension. You decide to talk to her, repeating the familiar, *Schuldigung, sprechen sie English?*

She turns and in nearly perfect English tells you that she speaks a little bit of English. You ask what she is sketching. She blushes a little, but then turns the pad towards you. She explains that she works for a jeweler, and she is designing jewelry.

That sounds like interesting work.

It can be. Especially when you get to work with diamonds. She says.

Why diamonds? You ask.

Well, in the beginning I did not like diamonds that much. I thought they were too, commercial. She explains. *But once you begin to work with them, they have the most wonderful vibration. Better than any other stone.*

You smile, offer your hand, and say, *I'm Dillon, can I get you another beer.*

Sure, she replies, *My name is Sehnka.*

In talking more about the vibration of things, Sehnka tells you that the best high energy spot in Austria is only a couple minutes walk from the restaurant. You ask her to explain, and she tells you that you just have to experience it.

Can you take me there, then?

Of course, Sehnka replies, *I told you, it is only around the corner. There is time for that, but let's finish our drinks.*

And so you stay at *Wrenkh* for another half an hour, talking about more of life's mysteries. You speak of simpler things too, of wine and beer and which is better when. You both prefer reds to whites and believe that wine should be at the base of the food pyramid. As you walk the plaza with her afterwards, you have that feeling, the one from childhood, of being weightless and walking on air. The exhilaration that something wonderful is happening.

As you reach Stephensplatz, Sehnka points to an area of brick that is a different color from the rest of the plaza. The brick forms the shape of a large rectangle with half-circles on each corner, looking vaguely like the top view of a small castle. She says, "Here it is. Not many people even know what this is. But the bricks outline the walls of an old chapel. I think it was built around 700 years ago. It was discovered when they were expanding the U-Bahn."

Can we go inside it? You ask.

I don't think it's open. It's almost eleven. But we can look.

Sehnka leads you down the stairs into the U-Bahn station where you first arrived two days ago. You turn left, round a wall and walk towards an obscure corner in which a single window is mounted. A plaque is affixed next to the window, with the title *Virgilkapelle*. The plaque explains that the chapel was built in 1250, but wasn't discovered in modern times until 1973 when the metro line was being built. Since the Thirteenth Century, the modern city was built up over the original city. The sign tell you that *Virgilkapelle* is only open from 11:30 a.m. to 4:30 p.m. on weekdays.

Disappointed, you start to climb back out to the plaza.

Sehnka grabs your hand and says, *Come on, there is something we can do.*

She leads you out to the middle of the brick outline. *Sit with me.* She says. And you both sit down cross-legged.

What are we doing? You ask, with a nervous but curious smile.

Okay, this may sound like I am crazy, but think of this spot as a giant diamond. Only this diamond is so big, we can use its vibration to change our own energy. She explained.

I don't feel anything. You mock, playfully.

Wait. She scolded.

We have different energy centers in our bodies just like we have different areas of taste in our mouths: this part for salty foods, that part for sweet things. So there are different centers for different emotions and activities. Each center is called a chakra, and it has its own vibration. The lower the center in your body, the lower the vibration. As you move up the body, the vibrations increase.

These chakras also connect us to the universal energy source, known as Chi in Eastern philosophy. There are seven basic chakras that line the spine, from your sacrum to the crown of your head. Each chakra has its own color, too. Because colors also have frequencies.

Then she talks you through a guided meditation and shows you how to bring energy from the ground into your body, through these energy centers. She tells you to absorb as much as your body will allow.

You do as she instructs, trying your best to imagine the things she describes. Then, without warning, the image of a dragon pops into your mind. With your eyes closed tight, the dragon swims through the air changing colors like a chameleon. You're a little freaked out by how clear the image is, and you almost open your eyes out of fear and surprise. But you resist. Then the dragon says to you without speaking: *If you do as I say, I can be your guide. An offering is requested, though. Tomorrow, at this place.*

When you finally open your eyes, Sehnka is staring at you, bemused. She begins to giggle. In spite of yourself, you start laughing too. Soon, you both fall over on the ground in hysterics. When you finally stop laughing, you ask, *What should we do now?*

Come on, I'll show you more things you won't find on your own.

And so you explore the city at night, and you learn all kinds of little Viennese secrets. You take dark, narrow corridors, see ancient relics, and learn about monuments to artists and political leaders. She leads you from hidden doorways to cathedral spires to gardens. You walk and talk for hours more.

Do you want another glass of wine? She asks, some time after 1 am. You nod and she says, *I know the perfect place. Come on, there's a shortcut.*

She leads you down a nearby alleyway, across a small courtyard, up a shallow flight of stairs and then through a narrow alley bordered by a stone wall on one side and several small cars on the other. On a corner, at a bend in the street, sits a small, one story, unassuming building with no exterior decoration. Only the words *santo spirito* appear over the doorway.

Although it seems very quiet from the outside, inside the place is buzzing with activity, exaggerated by the sounds of chamber music played at high volume. Sehnka tells you, *They play only classical and opera here. And they have the best wine list in the city.*

The crowd is fairly eclectic, most have the look and feel of the well-heeled artistic. Smart-looking and bespectacled, hair cut short and artfully disheveled. Dressed in black and gray, a cocktail dress or two, and a few worn sweaters and jeans. It may be fashionable, but it isn't a tourist bar. You get the feeling the clientele like it that way.

The seats at the bar are all full, so the two of you tour the rooms off the main bar, searching for a place to land. These rooms too are filled with people sitting, standing, talking, and smoking. You make your way back to the bar to order wine.

Just as you resign to standing, two spots open up at a far end.

The bartender hands you a wine list. You examine it, but it's no use. Beyond the category of *rôte vine*, you're clueless. You hand it to Sehnka. She yells to the bartender words you don't understand and he brings two glasses.

She asks what's in the journal you were writing in at the café. You tell her mostly just thoughts and notes on what you've seen. Sometimes poetry.

Really? Read a poem to me. She demands.

You flip through the pages for a minute and land on one you wrote the night before, while sitting on the plaza near Stephensdom, called *dragons*. You read it to her. When you finish, she laughs and says, *Read it again.* After you do, she reaches into her purse and says, *Okay, you have to close your eyes. I have a present for you.* When you close your eyes, she drapes something over your open palms. You open your eyes to a silk scarf, midnight blue, superimposed with different colored lizards.

Sehnka explains that earlier that morning she had gone shopping for a new scarf. She is friends with the owner of a little boutique on the plaza. She picked out a flowered scarf that she wanted and was ready to pay and leave when the owner pointed to this scarf and told her she thought she should have it also. She told her today is buy one get one free. For some reason, Sehnka felt like she should get them both. Now she understands why.

You look back to the poem in your journal, write a short note at the end of the page to your new friend, tear it out and give it to her. *This, then, must be yours. I must have written it for you.*

Thank you. Sehnka said. *I will keep this to remind myself of synchronicity.*

You talk on, order a second glass of wine and shout over the crescendo of the *aria* echoing against the thick walls. At last, Sehnka says she has to get home. You both finish your wine and relinquish your seats. You walk back to the plaza together through the chilly air. When you say goodbye, Sehnka hands you a business card and says, *My private atelier number is on there. When you come back to Vienna, you can stay with me, so you don't have to pay for a pension.*

And with that, you say goodnight.

⸺⸺

The next day, you eat breakfast in the sun-lit breakfast room at the pension. Over dark coffee with fresh cream and breakfast breads, you write out the details of the evening before in your journal. When you finish, you head for the plaza again.

Lighting a Gitanes on your way out the door, you pick up your shoulder pack and head for the weekly traders' market just outside the Ring. The world seems brighter today and you feel almost weightless again, as you glide over the cobblestones and through the plaza towards the market.

You are looking for a gift, the offering the dragon mentioned. It doesn't have to be expensive or grand, you will know it when you see it. Along the rows of merchants, you stop and admire the treasures and the trash. After wandering the market for a while, you finally glimpse your treasure. A small brass chalice. Call it a grail of sorts. You bargain with the merchant and walk away with it tucked safely inside your shoulder pack.

Then you retrace your steps from the night before to the small underground chapel. When you arrive at the entrance underground, you pause. You want to savor the anticipation. Like when you are about to kiss someone for the first time. The chapel is tucked away from the mainstream of Ubahn traffic. You read the name to yourself again—*Virgilkapelle*—and then pull open the door.

An old man with tufts of white hair on the sides of his head sits behind a narrow window on one side of the tiny entryway. Along one wall are shelves of artifacts apparently collected from the excavation of the chapel. You approach the narrow window. You hand the old man three marks. Without looking up, the man hands you a ticket.

Each item on the shelves has its own personal history posted with thumbtacks below it, but you can't read enough German to make any sense of what the little signs say. Besides, you are too eager to get to the other side of this wall. And so you leave the artifacts and carefully open the massive door to the chapel. No one is inside.

It feels like no one has been there for a while.

The door shuts behind you with a heavy thud. Amazing that this place was hidden away under this magnificent city for hundreds and hundreds of years. Locked up and untended. Hidden away even while Mozart played his masterpieces in the city above.

As you look up at the walls, you see a faded red cross. So faded it's almost pink. Its four arms are thick and all the same length. There is a small, simple altar in the center. Otherwise, the room is bare, stone walls and floor.

Taking your shoulder pack from your back, you reach in and remove the chalice, setting the bag on the ground. You feel a little silly as you place this gift, your own private grail, on the small altar. But you also can't deny the feeling of reverence here.

You sit down in the center of the chapel, a foot or two from the altar. And you try to remember the meditation Sehnka taught you the night before. As you start to open your chakras, instead of running the light up the channels on each side of your spine, the light seems to have a will of its own. It begins to spiral upwards. Like two snakes of light. Twisting in a double helix around your spine. This happens very quickly. You lose your sense of time and space. You see an image of an arm in a loose white shirt resting on an old desk. The hand moves frenetically. Ink stains the fingers. Notes and bars line the page. Then the notes turn to words. You read a single sentence: *You must make your music in a new way.* Then the image disappears. Only the pale outline of the cross remains.

You sit for a while longer, then pick up the shoulder bag, leaving the chalice, and open the big wooden door to the chapel. You thank the white tufts behind the narrow window. The old man responds, *You're welcome, son,* without looking up. You walk up out of the Ubahn station and into the sunlight of the plaza again.

WORDS: STUDY 5

we do not create words,
we discover them.
words have their own identities,

their own minds,
their own sense of purpose.
right and wrong,

left and right, true north.
we build fences to contain them,
they slip through the rails.

we lock them in their rooms,
they move through walls.
they hide under beds,

smoke cigarettes in bathrooms.
they eat junk food,
read dirty magazines.

fornicate with other words.
we call words to the table.
but they may not answer or they may not eat.

words play with their food.
if you kill their spirit, they die.
lying flat on the page, translucent.

the dna of words cannot be mapped.
there's only a probability of words.
words fold space. bend time. outrun light.

PHILLIP

Hey handsome. Didn't see you this weekend. Were you doing your best Kerouac and wooing bartenders in some other gin joint? I toss a coaster down on the bar and it spins to a resting place before one of the bar chairs.

Jillian. Jillian. That is why I keep coming back here, I guess. In a few words, you managed to make me feel talented, seductive, and missed. You sit down in front of the coaster.

That's what I'm here for, Phillip. How's the literary aspiration going? Feeling confident today? I say as I salt the rim of another glass and stack it on the pyramid with the others of its kind. I've already made the batch of strawberry margaritas to go with them.

Well, the aspiration is intact. But I don't know about the aspirant. He's a bit discouraged. You put your face in your hands.

What's the stumbling block du jour? I continue stacking.

I lost a whole weekend. You slide your hands up and down your face, twisting and distorting your features.

I thought you stopped drinking like that. I shake my head.

Funny. No, I remember it all. I just have no record of it. You pull a laptop out of your bag, along with a notepad filled with some scribbled notes, a stack of printed pages, and two pens.

Okay. Before we start playing this game of guess what happened, let's back up. Can I get you something? I place the last salt-rimmed glass on the stack.

Um, yeah. You scratch your head. *I'll have a pilsner and—a bowl of spicy tortilla soup.*

Alright, back to the riddle. I say, after I've entered your order.

I spent the weekend writing. Oh, it's almost too painful too tell— But basically I just wrote. Except for the occasional distraction: making coffee, scrounging for something to eat, making more coffee, thinking about sex, going to the store for more coffee. You know, the usual. You flip through your notes while you talk; then you decide on a page and set the notepad beside the computer.

So caffeine wasn't the problem, it seems. I start wiping down the espresso machine.

Well, it goes like that most of the weekend. I'm making some progress, but nothing to brag about. Then Sunday I fall into this groove and the story is just spilling onto the—paper, so to speak. You know, the screen paper. But I've barely eaten all day, so I come here around eight and I bang out six more pages and I'm just really in this zone. I don't leave here until after ten. Your voice takes on the sound and feel of frenetic typing.

Sounds good so far? I continue my spot cleaning.

Brace yourself, here comes the tragic part. You hold your hands straight out, palms open as if stopping traffic. *I start to shut down the laptop. The battery has gotten pretty low, but it should still be able to power down easily. The screen goes blank, but the power light doesn't go off. At first, I'm not that concerned, because, well, it's a computer, and it's anything but consistent. Anyway, I wait some more. Nothing. So I decide to just close it. I figure everything will be fine. I put it in the bag, pay the check, and go home.*

I sense some foreshadowing. I stop polishing.

Yeah. I get home and plug it in and reboot. But it has to go through scan check, because I've run the battery down, instead of shutting it down normally. Everything comes back on. I log on, check e-mail, and Dillon sends me a text. We chat awhile. We drink a beer together, me in the States, him in Europe. Dillon wrote something that made me remember I didn't back up the last few pages of the work. So I pull up the chapter while I'm still chatting with him and back it up without really looking. Then I realize I'm looking at a blank page. I tell Dillon I have to go, sign off, and desperately start looking for the file anywhere on my computer. No backup anywhere. I run a search of the hard drive. Nothing. Completely erased from memory. As if it never happened. Your hands are flying all over in illustration of your state of mind.

Ouch. What's the damage? I wince.

Around fifteen pages I think. Thought it was more, but I found the beginning of the chapter that I managed to back up.

Hmmm. The words cloud-back-up come to mind. I'm no help.

Thanks. You're not the first to point out that solution with piercing hindsight. I think our friend Dillon fell off his chair laughing when I told him.

Well, for what it's worth, I think it's a chance for you to flex your creative muscle. Show the gods they can't beat you so easily. Just think of it like serendipity. Usually, I would bask in your misery at a time like this, but I can tell you're genuinely pained by the incident.

Isn't serendipity finding something you didn't know you wanted?"

Something like that-

Well, I've lost something. I haven't found something. That line of thinking is not going to get you anywhere as a writer.

Yes, but its only because you lost those words that you now have the opportunity to find something you weren't looking for. I explain neatly. What was this lost chapter about? Or can you tell me?

What else? The same thing people have been writing about since Beowolf. The great mystery. The thing that has caused wars and the collapse of empires. You resort to grand gestures.

Greed?

Come on, you know the world is a sucker for lost love, for heartbreak. You take a swallow of your beer and turn on the computer.

Do you really think love is ever lost? I set down your soup on the bar.

Yes. Happens all the time. Where've you been? You pick up the spoon and hold it poised.

I don't know about that. I don't think it's lost. I think it becomes part of you. Love changes us and the world. I stop cleaning and take down a glass from the salted stack. Then I fill half the glass with fresh margarita and sample it.

If it isn't really a loss, then why is it so painful? You were never one for allowing a conversation to end too quickly. You'll take any side just to keep it interesting. You lift the spoon and blow.

I think that has to do with our expectations. We're sold too much as kids. And then our whole lives, TV, movies, magazines, and fairy tales delicately and deceptively feed us this unrealistic fantasy.

I don't think most of us are supposed to love just one person our whole lives. I think that's a rare phenomenon. I think people are supposed to take each other to some place and then move on to the next adventure. But far too many people get stuck somewhere along the way living Thoreau's lives of quiet desperation.

But what about true love, Jillian? Your contrarian nature this time has taken you far astray from your traditional path of cynicism.

What about it? I shrug, taking another sip of my recent alchemy.

Doesn't true love exist? You sound almost believable as a romantic. You finally put the spoon in your mouth.

Well, yes, but I think it's really rare. But also, who says you can't have true love with more than one person? Do you think there is only one true love for you? I continue, still nursing my margarita along with my theory of love.

I don't know. I've known a few women. But that feeling, that excitement, that overwhelming sense of joy that I believe is real love I've only known once. And it was for such a short period of time. What if that was it? What if that was my share of that feeling, whatever you want to call it. Somehow in this old-fashioned game of wits and rhetoric, you find yourself more exposed than you expected.

Have you been practicing this tragic writer persona for so long you believe it? You've been in love more than once. I know. I've been there. The thing is, memory twists things. Time sifts things through our romantic filter of the world.

And you're still in your twenties. Barely, I'll grant you. But where'd you get this hopeless view of the world that makes you think you'll

144

never experience love again? What's with you and Dillon lately? I'm beginning to wonder if I'm the one that's lost it.

Maybe you're right. You appear to have forgotten whatever strategy took you to this side of the debate.

Of course I'm right. It's like the book you're writing. Why are you doing that? Don't you believe in it? And in the ones that will come after? Would you be doing it if you didn't?

Part of me believes it. Most of the time. I guess that's why I keep on. But there are other times when I'm certain I'm not talented enough. Or lucky enough.

That's the trick isn't it? To get up the next day and keep writing even when you doubted yourself the day before. Love is no different. Why are you pursuing little miss copper sunshine if you don't believe true love exists? I pick up the rocks glass again and take another sip, as if to say, *check.* Though I may have jumped the gun.

I'm surprised at you, now. It's a little three-letter word spelled s-e-x. Maybe you've heard of it. Your tone says you've regained your footing and are proclaiming checkmate. Perhaps that too is a little premature.

Cynics are just people who are searching for reasons to justify being unhappy. Being a cynic doesn't mean that you're interesting. There isn't a theory or a belief system or a religion or a novel or a relationship that you can't punch holes in *if you try hard enough. But why do you want to spend your energy that way?* I'm getting ready to plant my victory flag.

You aren't ready to concede defeat. *Does that mean what I've often suspected: That everything is bullshit?* You've come full circle. And now you're able to fall back into character. As if you've planned the whole thing.

If that's how you want to see it. Or it could be that you only try to punch holes in any given thing because you don't understand it. And that scares the shit out of you. It could be that your holes are the things that are illusionary, and the world actually makes perfect sense. It could be that the universe is smarter than you, and you just don't know enough yet. Checkmate.

This is too heavy a conversation for lunch. You resign yourself and turn instead to the laptop screen, click the mouse and open the fractured chapter.

I think we can agree on that. How's your soup? I tip the rocks glass.

REMBRANDT: STUDY 3

the painter
borrowed money
to give it away.

the painter
knew the things
society demanded

and the things
it would not forgive
were the same.

the painter lived richly.
the painter died poor.
the words only grew stronger.

MAGGIE

Your reality is a bit fuzzy right now. Like the dreams you used to have where you thought you were awake and going about your morning, only to awaken and discover that you were late for school. And then you would spend the rest of the day trying to sort out exactly which thing was really happening, which had happened, and which was a dream.

You close the laptop and stare at the blank pad of yellow paper, trying to imagine words on the pages. The yellow pad is your road map. The court has a tendency to focus on completely obscure matters, so staying on message requires diligent planning. The words you pick are as important as the lines of a cartographer. In the past, a condemned man's life would hang from a rope. At this moment, a condemned man's life dangles from the string of words you'll chart on this paper. They must not only be carefully chosen, but written in big print, lines skipped to help keep your place during arguments. You know these issues well enough to recite them from memory. But you will over-prepare so you don't open the briefcase of memory in the middle of court and find it empty.

There are twenty-one claims of error in your petition, but only two are linchpin issues: Mercado's trial lawyer made unreasonable errors and the State hid key evidence. This is where you'll try to steer the Court's attention.

The first claim, involving the trial lawyer, is simple: Mercado was pressured into pleading guilty. The lawyer told him if he entered a guilty plea before the prosecution filed a notice of intent to seek the death penalty, they'd be unable to ask for it. This was a fundamental error. Primarily because that isn't the law. The trial lawyer testified that he took the rule from a procedure notebook he received at a death penalty seminar. But he was unable to produce the notebook at a subsequent hearing. Mercado later tried to withdraw the plea, but the Court denied his attempt, calling his self-styled motion a rogue document, since he was represented by counsel.

The lawyer also claimed he was prevented from taking the matter to trial by Mercado himself, who had insisted on a defense inconsistent with the evidence. Mercado denied this was true and signed an affidavit accordingly. And finally there's the American Bar Association rules for capital cases which forbid lawyers in capital cases from pleading their clients straight up, without first securing some benefit of the bargain.

Of course, the trial court refused to take Mercado's word over that of his trial lawyer and found in any case that the evidence supported his plea of guilt. (You remember Big Bird.) Unless a trial lawyer is willing to fall on the sword, it doesn't usually happen differently. Sometimes even that isn't enough.

The second issue is known as a *Brady* violation, after a U.S. Supreme Court case of the same name. In layman's terms, this means the State's prosecutor hid key evidence. After Mercado's sentencing, it came to light that one of his co-defendant's statements had been "lost" by the State. The co-defendant admitted the stabbing to the police and also named the person who held down the deceased during the struggle. That person was not Mercado, but a third suspect who was originally questioned by police and then fled the jurisdiction. The statement had been recorded.

But the State had enough evidence to nail the co-defendant without the confession. And the prosecutor knew that if the statement surfaced it would only complicate things (i.e., prove your client's lack of involvement in the actual murder). The court would be forced to sever the trials or the statement would have to be redacted to take out any reference to Mercado, who had not given any statement and was still protected by the Fifth Amendment. Because the State wanted both Mercado and his co-defendant, and because the other guilty party had fled to Timbuktu, they buried the statement.

The problem for the State is that conspiracies are harder to pull off than people think. There are always paper trails. These days, electronic one. And there are always things like disgruntled former employees. In reading through the trial record and the voluminous other documents that came with discovery, you found a reference to the confessional statement. It was in a memo buried in a stack of otherwise yawn-inducing paper.

For obvious political reasons, the trial court refused to reverse the conviction. It ruled instead that the statement was inadmissible hearsay, and it accepted the State's argument that the failure to turn it over was simply excusable neglect. Harmless error.

It helps to rehearse your arguments out loud. And you've taken to coming in during off hours and practicing on me. Sometimes I become familiar enough with your cases to give parts of the argument myself. In this case, I've learned that the problem with the lower court's ruling is that the co-defendant's statement, although hearsay, was admissible because it's against his own interest.

The absence of the statement then (along with the encouragement of trial counsel) forced a guilty plea. The trial court committed reversible error in not allowing Mercado to withdraw the plea.

That's all it takes, a couple of errors, a single obfuscation, and a man innocent of first-degree murder sits on death row. Yes, it happens. And not just in the movies.

You put the yellow pad in the box with the other materials for your argument. You put the lid on the box, sit back in your chair and look out the window. The lake begins to disappear behind the falling curtain of darkness. You think about how other things are disappearing in your life. First, your faith in the legal system. Then your feelings for Christophe. Now the café is in danger. You hope Mercado isn't next.

DILLON

We all spiral.
Chase our tails.

In the illuminations which visit us
in between the cobblestones of our past,
distant planets align
to send us a glimmer

of who we are. Down deep
in the indestructible soil of memory

the universe wants desperately
for us to hear the voice
of the sacred antelope of Africa;
to see the last painted oxen

on the Viennese wall of time;
to tell stories inside granite caves

in a language yet to be invented.
But the fire of becoming
eats the worm of understanding
until I fall back here.

Drinking passionately
at the ember on the far end

of this cigarette of time,
remembrance does not quench my thirst.
Still I awake as a serpent
in a chair in an old café in München.

Where Rilke reflects upon the hidden passion
of a pacing, caged panther.

Many years ago. Yesterday. Right now.
I have to ask him for a light.

DILLON

You stroll up from the underground train station and make your way through the München spring wind towards the university. Your attention is caught by a used bookstore. A sign in its window announces it carries books in English. You turn left into the store and climb a short set of stairs towards the cluttered shelves. Your eyes scan the stacks, landing on an orange spine. You slide it from between its tightly-packed neighbors. Its cover reads: *Serpent of Fire*.

You pick up the book and turn it over to read that it is about something called *kundalini* and higher states of consciousness. You take it to the counter and ask how much it costs. The bookstore clerk quotes you a price way above what you expect to pay for a book in a used bookstore. The owner explains it's expensive because it is an import—from America. You think about the irony as you hand over twice the book's price in the US.

Around the corner you find a salon more than 125 years old, where Rilke, Lenin, and Strauss used to play pool. You order a local beer and pull your new book out of your shoulder pack. The book references Carl Jung and Krishnamurti on the subject. You read that the awakening of this kundalini energy in the body is often like two snakes of light arising from the base of the spine and spiraling, like DNA, up to the brain. And also that the medical symbol of the two snakes wrapping vertically around a staff actually comes from imagery of kundalini awakenings.

You mark the page with an U-bahn pass and set the book on the table for a minute. You light a cigarette and sit back in your chair. Coincidence is a word we've invented to explain something we can't explain. You write notes in your journal. You want this moment of synchronicity and revelation to last, and at the same time you know that it can't.

After another cigarette, you pick up the book and begin to read again. You learn about the connection between kundalini and sexual energy. You also learn that there are many accounts of madness that occur from the awakening of kundalini, including schizophrenia.

You stay at the Salon for another hour, reading about the various reported experiences of the different mystics who wrote about their kundalini experiences. When you can't absorb any more, you pay for the beer and go for a stroll outside.

≡

By 8 pm, you are cold and tired of walking. You need to sit down to a warm meal. Wandering down Turkenstrausse, you come upon a café called *La Bohème*. Unable to resist Italian food no matter where you are in the world, you enter and are greeted by dim lighting, long stemmed candles, and friendly staff. You take a seat at one of the long tables near the front windows.

The server's small build, short dark hair, and dark eyes cause her to pass for Italian, even if she isn't. She asks if she can bring you a drink. Because you can't read the menu, you ask her to choose a red wine for you. She says the house wine is actually very good and suggests a half carafe. You accept.

Another woman arrives shortly with a carafe of water and a small basket of breads. You unfold the cloth, tear off a piece of peasant bread and dip it in the olive oil before you reach for your shoulder pack. The way all the puzzle pieces are fitting together on this journey gives you the sense that you are being pulled inside of a life for a change. That maybe there are other forces at play.

The dark-haired waitress returns to check on you. Simply professional until now, she turns friendly when she sees what you are reading. She asks whether you are enjoying the book. Since you had never heard of kundalini until just a few hours ago, you are even more surprised. *You know about this?* You ask.

I wouldn't say that I know about it. But I am interested. She replies, then has to check on another table. When she returns, you question how she knows about this thing. *Same way as you, probably.* She answers.

You mean you experienced this? You ask.

Then she does something unexpected. She sits down at the table with you and her professional exterior melts away. She takes on the look of an old friend who has just joined you for dinner as she responds, *No, but I have a teacher and I am studying things like this.*

For how long? You ask.

Two years or so. She replies. And then asks, *And what about you?*

I'm not sure. But I think so. I think this just happened to me. You answer, as honestly as you can.

How can you not know? She asks, bluntly.

Well, I suppose it's like how I feel right now. You begin. *I feel like I know you. Like we are friends and have known each other for a while.*

Her face, so serious and intense before, softens. *I know what you mean. I was supposed to meet you tonight. To serve you dinner and ask you about your book.*

The two of you talk for another minute, when she is about to go tend to another table, you confess, *I want to talk with you.*

We are talking. She smiles.

What I mean is, when there is more time.

I don't work until five tomorrow, but I have lunch plans. You can call me in the afternoon. She instructs, before getting up to tend to her other tables. Later, when she brings the check, a slip of paper with her number is also on the tray.

The next day, you can hardly wait until noon. You busy yourself with a long early morning walk through the center of town and down along the riverbanks. You stop at a sidewalk café for milchkaffee and fresh croissants while you try in vain to read a München newspaper. You tour a Van Gogh exhibit. And finally, around 1 pm you take the U3 to Marienplatz. You walk up the stairs, find the nearest phone, insert your Munich card and dial the numbers written on the slip of paper.

After three rings, a male voice answers, *Hallo.* You never asked if she was in a relationship. The last thing you want is to create a situation she will have to explain. You almost hang up. But at the last second, you say, *Yes, I'm looking for Lucia. My name is Dillon.* The voice says something back you don't understand, and you hear a muffled call.

When she picks up the phone and says hello, you are still wondering if you did the right thing. She directs you to a little bar just around the corner from where you are and says she'll be there in a few minutes. Then, before you hang up, she says, *Dillon—*

Yes— You reply, a little anxious.

I am happy you called.

You find the place easily. You scan the room, but she is not there yet. You sit down and order a milchkaffee. As the waitress brings the coffee, the small form of Lucia opens the door to the café and light from outside spills in, illuminating her from behind.

You rise to greet her. She smiles as she approaches, placing her hands on the outside of your arms and gently kissing each side of your face. Your conversation begins clumsily.

She asks, *Are you having fun on your holiday?*

There is so much to see, you reply, *But I think I have never had a better time in my life.*

Where all have you been?

More than I can remember right now, but I've taken good notes. I've been to Berlin, Prague, Vienna, and now here. So many stories. Even the trains have stories.

I wanted to go to Italy. But I decided against it so I could spend more time in Vienna. Funny how things work out. If I'd gone to Italy, I wouldn't have met you. So I guess I was supposed to meet you. What do you think?

I don't know the words for it in English. But I trust you. Lucia began to explain. *Being with you takes no effort. Like being pulled in a wagon.*

I'm kind of a cynic. And I don't like a lot of people. Which affords me the luxury of knowing when I like someone. And I definitely like you. So tell me about your teacher.

I'm not sure what you want to know. Lucia answers.

I don't know, either, I suppose. What do you study?

Mostly mediation. Even though she says she trusts you, she is not very willing to elaborate.

Ok, let me ask this. Are there things in the teachings which are hard for you to swallow? But before she can answer, you continue. What I mean is, I find there is dogma attached to most things I encounter. Take Buddhism. The essence of Buddhism, as I understand it, is for everyone to find their own path. It is supposed to be a religion of no religion. There is a story that the Buddha once spent several days in conversation with a leader of another religion. At the end of their visit, the leader confessed to the Buddha that he wanted to leave his own religion and follow the Buddha. The Buddha told the leader to return to his people, that he wasn't looking for followers... I love that story. But, I think modern Buddhism is not true to that concept.

I agree. It is very confusing. Lucia confirmed.

I've always been able to see through the gaping holes in religion. I have sought out teachers and books and so-called alternative beliefs out of a long-standing distrust of organized religion. But I always find hidden agendas in those alternative ways as well.

Well, I do question. And I definitely understand what you say.
Lucia adds.

Krishnamurti said the truth is a pathless land. You add.

*I think truth must be like fingerprints. Different for every person.
And, I've found that as soon as I think I've found something, it
always slips away.* She says with a measure of frustration and
disappointment.

You want to be able to give her answers instead of simply
complaining about their absence. But because you can't, you
say, *I distrust anyone who claims to be enlightened.*

Didn't the Buddha claim to be enlightened? She asks.

*Well, I wasn't there. But maybe what happened to the Buddha
under the Bhodi tree was simply the beginning of enlightenment.
Take Jesus for example. While he may have been a being out of
his time, he displayed human emotions and flaws. Anger with
the tax collectors in the temple, weeping in the garden before he
was to be crucified. I think we've been programmed to believe
that enlightenment and spirituality are something they are not.
It shouldn't surprise us that they have been commercialized, like
everything else.*

My turn for a question: If all the answers are inside, which I think I believe, then why do we need each other so desperately? Lucia posits.

Honestly, I don't know. Perhaps the universal laws that govern how things work and why are beyond our comprehension. I believe in the paradox. Things that seem contradictory may not be. You answer.

I have this theory that I think life is organized in circles. That there really is no beginning and no end to things. Take Finnegan's Wake, James Joyce started it in the middle of the story and ended it in the middle of the story. He used a series of dreams as his literary tool, which was perfect, because dreams often don't make any linear sense. If there are no beginnings and no ends, then there are no absolutes, no black and no white, only perpetually differing gradations of gray that turn back into the same colors over infinity.

I lost you somewhere I think. Lucia stops you.

Let me try it this way. If everything exists on a circle, then there is no right or wrong, no good or bad, only different sides of the same circle, ever moving and evolving towards each other. You draw a circle over and over on your napkin as you try to explain.

You see. That is hard to swallow. If that is so, then it doesn't matter what we do. It doesn't matter if I am nice to you, if I make love to you, or if I kill you.

I'm not an expert at existentialism, but I think you're right, it doesn't matter. That's the other side of the circle. The paradox. It does matter, because it matters to you. Because your soul is working on something, and that's more important. It matters and it doesn't. Both exist on the same circle at the same time. You pause for a moment.

I think you are probably right, but it is still confusing. It means that there is no right direction for us to take. Lucia protested.

Well, that's not exactly what I meant. There is a right direction for us to take. It is the one our hearts tell us to take. I know, that sounds a little cheesy. But it's the one that feels right. Sometimes it's the easiest, sometimes the hardest. You sip your coffee.

What if we can't decide something? What if nothing feels right? Lucia challenged.

I don't know. Maybe Camus was right. He said that we will never live if we are always looking for the meaning of life.

You both order more coffee and you tell her of your experiences over the past few weeks. About Sehnka and the *dragons* poem. She asks if you kept a copy of the poem and have it with you. You pull out the journal and start flipping through it, through the receipts and the u-bahn tickets and the museum pamphlets and the pages scribbled with words and sketches. Your hand lands on a page you haven't looked at for several weeks. It is the scribbled writing of the old painter from *Cafe Eins* in Berlin. There are four things written on the page. They are: Bauernmarkt (underlined twice); Belverdere: Gust Klimt; Stephens Dom: (with an arrow to) Cellar; and Wienerschnitzel (underlined four times). You never had a Wienerscnitzel while in Vienna. All the other things, other people directed you to.

Over the next few days, you and Lucia spend more time together. You meet her for coffee in the afternoon and you eat in her restaurant at night. Twice you walk her home late at night after her shift. On the evening before you are going to leave to fly back to the states, you walk her home again, continuing your discussions about life and how to live it. When you arrive at her door, neither of you are ready for goodbye. You both stand there feeling awkward. Finally, you lean towards her and say in a whisper, *I'm going to kiss you.*

In the early morning you rise and walk back down Marien Strausse in the half-light. You step in a puddle of water in the street, sending the sunlight tumbling off its trampoline of glass and rolling over the cobblestones.

≡

This same night, you dream. Of waking under an indigo sky. Lying flat against the parched earth. Light blue clouds, broken from their shells and whipped across the vast plane of the sky, lie just beyond your reach. At your feet, golden grasses wave in perfect synchronicity with the wind. A lone tree holding only a handful of leaves stands unapologetically to your left. Its bleached skeleton reaching up to the heavens, remembering what it was to feel water seep through its fingers.

On the horizon, daubs of green paint remind you that the clouds sometimes keep their promises. Beyond this, swift and slender beasts dart across the plain, each guided by two graceful antennae. They mock your slumber.

You yawn, stretch, and push yourself upright. And then, a ghost appears. She slinks into your field of vision on all fours. As casually as the wind, as sure as the sun, she moves your way. A thin white coat covers the sinewy limbs of a trained assassin, but her ice blue eyes cast a benevolent gaze. A moment later you can feel her breath on your skin. This is no mirage.

This is Timbavati. This is the soul of the world.

WORDS: STUDY 6

words must be seduced.
a little candlelight,

belgian chocolates.
french champagne,
asian silk.

red petals,
whispered verse.

there's no
sure way
to make them come.

no matter how
hard you work.

PHILLIP

I've been so naive. You complain. *All this time thinking I knew how to write.*

The fog around your head is so thick fish could swim in it.

Mr. Kent, what happened, are all the phone booths out of order?

I have a new idea for a book. I think I'll call it Little Insipid Thoughts. Whadda you think?

Well, satire is in. I answer.

I know you are here seeking sympathy; you want me to feel sorry for you. Instead, I'm elated. Watching you struggle gives me a sense of peace. Partly because I think it's foreign territory. But also because it means you've finally gotten your hands muddy. You're wading around in the muck of self-exploration. It's impossible to write without finding out something about yourself. If you are doing it right. If you are being honest.

There is something missing from my writing. I feel like it isn't real. It's still the Velveteen Rabbit, still the wooden boy. I don't believe in it, yet.

That is why fail you do.

Thank you, Master Yoda.

I turn to the stacks, consider the wisdom there, and pull down an appropriate volume. I pour the words into small glasses, place one before you, and sample the text myself before returning the volume to the shelf.

I thought I had the gift of alchemy. I heard other people grumble about writer's block and lack of confidence. The wadded paper and discarded manuscripts littering their lives. And I would smugly turn a bored ear. I'm paying for it now.

No wonder you're having trouble, even your complaint is a cliché. You sound like so many Casanovas who—when skin deep in the sheets and stricken with stage fright—offer the tired, *but that's never happened to me.* As if life was something that happened only to other people, as if only the rest of us suffered the indignities of the flesh.

Perhaps that's what arrogance costs. I offer.

How long must I tithe to pay for this sin? You cross yourself and lift your glass to your lips, as if it's a communion chalice.

It *seems to me that the problem is not one of penance, but patience. You need to find your voice, Phillip. It can only get to the page through you. You are the doorway, but it needs help. It's wandering around outside your house. You hear it every now and then, but you haven't let it inside yet.*

I'm open to suggestions. You finish off your chapter and scoot the empty page towards me with a nod. I pour more ink from the same volume.

In baseball they tell you never to take your eye off the ball. But in writing sometimes distraction is helpful. I explain.

You're saying I have to fall in love in order to find my voice? You swallow the words.

There is the usual sarcasm behind your words still, but it's tempered with humility. You're not used to grappling with the ethereal.

It's like I've been saying.

You can't hear the voice right now. But I'm pretty sure you're tuned in to the sound of beauty knocking. If you can hear her and open the door, your voice might be able to slip inside at the same time and finally make its way to the page.

What if I've been wrong all along? What if I was wrong about myself and I just don't have what it takes to wrestle these words and pin them to the page?

Maybe I have underestimated your crisis of faith. *What is a word, anyway? If you look closely enough. Isn't it like an atom? An illusion of weight and strength? A probability of power? By itself, I'm not sure it's anything. Until there's a voice to speak it.*

I hold up my glass, you touch yours to it. Words spill over the rim as the glasses meet. But they don't make any sound.

LOVE: STUDY 5

love is not an anchor.
love is the sailboat
cut adrift in the storm.
love is the wave
crashing on your bow.
love is the sheets of rain

blinding your horizon.
love is the wind
ripping your sail

and howling
the invisible moon.
love is the shattered storm cloud

drenching everything beneath.
love is the torn canvas
dancing above your head.

MAGGIE

Do you think my costume fits? You ask.

You arrive at *rembrandt* around four, dressed in a suit. I'm leaning over the *Times* and pretending I'm making respectable progress with Friday's crossword. The café is quiet. Clean and quiet. Floor swept. Wood oiled. Tables set. Same thing at the bar. Glasses washed. Bottles wiped. Beers on ice. But your question scatters my orderly thoughts. I look up, trying not to let on that I have no idea what you're talking about.

I woke up this morning and I was in court and I couldn't figure out whose clothes I was wearing.

One of those this is not my beautiful house *things?*

You could say.

Sambuca?

Ok.

I turn to the shelves behind me, take down a tiny version of a champagne glass and drop three coffee beans into the bottom. I reach for the bottle, turn it upside down, and watch the clear liquid flow unhurriedly from the stainless-steel spout, over the beans and almost to the rim. I place it just in front of you.

Salud! I exclaim.

The powerful anise expands as it enters your throat, opening your senses. You close your eyes to savor the alchemy.

So, why the identity crisis? I start to put the bottle on the shelf but it doesn't seem to want to go back just yet. It takes a detour near the rim of my coffee cup, and I'm obliged to let it have its way.

Do you know that feeling of hearing a song, and there's just something about it. You start playing it over and over again. It feels so good you try to crawl right inside it. But no matter how many times you play it or how loudly you sing along, you can't actually get inside.

This is pretty abstract thinking for someone who spends her days in the relentless pursuit of logic. I consider my words, sip my coffee first for emotional support. *Separation is an illusion, you know. Everything is connected already. Which is why the song can't make you whole. Any more than another person can make you whole.*

Well the illusion feels pretty fucking real. You skillfully extract a coffee bean with a toothpick and put it on your tongue.

I hear you, girl. Is all I can come up with. I'm going to need sustenance for this conversation, so I put in an order for pasta chips.

I just can't stand the distance anymore. It feels unbridgeable. Is that a word?

If you want it to be. I'm not being aloof. There are people who would scorn your concerns as being petty. You poor, highly educated, well-paid white girl. Really, with all the suffering, poverty, starvation, disease, war, natural disasters and countless unthinkable ways humans treat each other daily, feeling disconnected from a song is not at the top of the list. But that doesn't make it any less universal. There are all kinds of ways to starve to death.

Maybe I'm just really confused about how it is the world continues on at this pace. About how people have done it for generations. Made it work. Or if they have. You twist the small glass back and forth on the bar between your finger and thumb. The pendant lights above the bar strike the glass. Some reflect in precise, mathematically calculable angles, others get muddled in the syrupy liquid.

I think it's called being overwhelmed. I say. Sounds like you need a change of scenery. And some room to breathe.

I know the world is a big place. Actually, that's part of the problem. It's too big. Isn't it enough that we are all just wandering around barely holding on to that little niche of information that we almost understand? Isn't it enough that the questions are limitless, not to mention the answers? Isn't it enough that science and technology have already exceeded our ability for personal growth and awareness by light years? You lift the Sambuca to your lips again and pour half of it down your throat.

The world is as big as your thoughts of it. Maybe you should take a vacation and go somewhere that plays by different rules. Go to Spain, where every day the whole country shuts down—right in the middle of the day—and they don't return to work until they feel like it, 6, 7, 8 o'clock sometimes. Go to an island where the only two things to do are lay in a hammock and read or walk down the beach to the fish taco stand. There are many, many places left in the world where the American clock doesn't set the pace.

Sometimes people bring up things to talk about which are not the things they really want to talk about. This is another one of those times. Fortunately, the snacks just arrived from the kitchen.

Do you think couples are ever truly happy? You come clean.

No. I set the basket between us.

Wow. Really? Your face drops wide open.

I mean, I think happiness is really, really relative. I sprinkle on extra Parmesan and dip one of the warm chips into the marinara.

What do you mean? That it is situational? You follow my lead.

I mean that couples I've known who are the happiest are those who have given up the fairy tale. They've figured out that love is something very different from the big-screen version... And those who are just blissfully stupid. But I don't think you're that lucky. I reach back into the basket.

I feel like there's just a lot of damage floating around. In this endless search for ourselves in someone else, we cause a lot of damage. We're all just out there whirling around like bargain shoppers on red tag day, desperately trying on this shoe and that one, looking for the perfect fit. But in the meantime, we're just stretching and tearing and scuffing each other up, until nobody is untouched. Nobody looks or feels the way they were supposed to. You finish the Sambuca and slide the glass my way.

I motion for a refill, but you shake it off and nod to the wine rack.

This all goes back to the myth of separation. I say as I turn to the rack. What I'm saying is that you're already whole. I slide a bottle out and peel back the foil. You watch with some anticipation as the corkscrew starts its ritualistic descent.

Why don't I know that? Why doesn't everyone? And if that's true, love doesn't make any sense then. Why is it around if we don't need it? Why haven't we learned something from all the years this has been going on? It's like we're all out there with our eyes taped shut, stumbling around in the dark, crushing each others' toes, bumping into walls.

Careful mixing your metaphors. Beer or wine, not both. I extract the cork, pull down a glass, and pour a little taste.

Why do we keep doing it? You manage to squeeze in another question before you raise the glass.

Maybe we're just optimistic that the next pair will fit. Even if they're scuffed and torn. Maybe they'll be so comfortable, it won't matter.

You nod and I fill the glass, stopping a little above the proper mark.

I can't believe you're advocating that we should settle for comfortable. Anyway, I just can't bring myself to go shopping again.

I'm not saying you should settle for anything. But sometimes the best shoes are the ones that are a bit worn. I sip my coffee, but due to a hole in my chin, it spills on my white shirt. I reach for the bar wand and spray some soda water on a towel to soak the stain free. Then I have a thought.

Wouldn't it be nice if life were more like a restaurant? Here, if you get stains on something, you just take some soda water, soak it into a towel, and the stains magically disappear.

THREE PARTS

THE PAINTER

The painter stepped back from the easel and lifted a corner of his blue linen smock to clean the tips of his fingers. The color blue found a comfortable home in the rooms of his great house. Blue is the color of the spirit. He believed spirit infused every thing, and that all things were illuminated from within. If you could begin to understand this, the painter might receive you. Even then, he would only talk with you as he sketched or as he walked the alleyways to pick out new colors. The painter did not waste time.

When the doctor came in, it was just past dawn. The painter was busy sketching the design of a new picture. He used a simple brown, thinned down to near transparency, to trace the shapes and shadows of a world in which he was already dissolved, even as he was inventing it. He stood working in the day before yesterday's clothes, creating color and shape as if he were in a trance. And yet, each brush stroke was deliberate, considered.

Painters, like sculptors, tend to develop a signature technique. A routine they follow. This allows them to train apprentices who eventually take over much of the work. While the painter had apprentices from time to time whom he could teach certain things about painting, he could not teach them to paint like him. The painter did not follow a certain line. There was no repetition. He employed not one technique, but every technique, even inventing new ones along the way. Like fingerprints, each painting had its own identity that had to be discovered, its own secrets to be uncovered. He never allowed himself to fall back on answers he had found before.

The doctor stood in the doorway to the room for twenty minutes, maybe more. His arrival was announced, but either the painter had not heard, or simply thought it not a detail he need acknowledge.

The painter was made of sturdy material and could work for two days on end, not stopping to eat or sleep. Those around him, though—his wife, his children—did not share his constitution. The painter's wife was sick, but despite his keen powers of observation and the loss of two children already, the painter did not see death loitering near her bed. The doctor could find no convincing reason to tell him. He would know soon enough. And in the meantime, knowing would not change the fact of it.

When eventually he was made aware of her decline, he did something rare. He cleaned his brushes and covered his work. He closed the door to the studio and went to their bedroom where he sat with her for days until she passed. When finally he picked up his brushes again, he was still dressed in black.

LOVE: STUDY 6

187

love does not come lightly.
love will not go unheard.
love does not take a number.

love will not do as you say.
love cannot be organized
and filed.

love is not assigned a number.
love is not an essay.
love dies on the shelf.

love is poetry.
without ordered rhyme
or verse.

DILLON

Well, I mean, under normal circumstances, I'm disoriented. I sometimes forget where I am or what season it is. I have to think for a minute. I've been lost in thought in my own house before, where for I split second I think what room is this? So you can imagine how it is to wake up every few days in another country.

You've been back for two days. But apparently you've done little else besides sleep. And try to retrace your steps. To make yourself believe the adventure was real. To ponder how quickly we can move between places which seem worlds apart.

Coming home is always a mixed bag of feelings: lingering excitement and sudden loss. There is an ambivalence between wanting to share your stories and wanting to keep them to yourself. You are at once aware of life's possibilities and its limitations.

I went to Africa a few years ago to work on a farm. I was there only six months, but coming back to the States was like waking from a dream. That moment of disorientation before you scratch your head in disappointment and then get up, brush your teeth, put on your clothes and start your day.

On the way home, I didn't realize how unprepared I was to return to the modern world. I had read and researched and prepared myself as well as I could for Kenya. For the drastic differences in the culture, the way of life. The irony is there was nothing I could do to prepare myself for coming home. For rush hour traffic, lines of people, and stacks of useless stuff, shrink-wrapped and stacked to the ceiling in the supermarket. For billboards and magazines and televisions and commercials and computers and gas stations and convenience stores. For shoe sales and car lots and electrical wires and airplanes streaming their blinking messages across the sky. I wasn't ready for that. Which is strange of course, because I've known these things my whole life.

The day after I came back, I was standing in the grocery store with a bottle of red wine in one hand and a fresh baguette in the other, when suddenly I was overwhelmed. I felt dizzy, unsure of my feet. For a moment I knew what it must be like to be schizophrenic. I could hear every sound in the building. I could hear every conversation, every footstep, every beep of every register, every rattle of every grocery cart, every jingling of every car key, every child's desperate plea for candy or toaster pastries, every scribble of every pen. I became paralyzed and my hands went slack. The baguette slid from its paper sheath and the bottle of wine shattered on the concrete floor. I woke up to find I wasn't dreaming and ran out of the store.

Re-entry is never easy. I remind you. *You remember what happened to me when I came back from Africa."*

It's worse than that. You insist calmly.

That was pretty bad...

Well, it's different anyway. You hesitate for just a minute. Then you look up and explain, in an almost matter-of-fact tone, *I see things that aren't there. People and animals and even inanimate things. I'll turn to look at them again, there'll be nothing there.*

And I see other things wrong. Like words that are actually different words. I'll read a sentence in the newspaper. And I'll think it's odd, so I'll re-read it and it will say something completely different than what I read the first time. I'll have to read it a third time. On the way over here, I almost killed myself because I went through a green light that was actually red.

Maybe it's just jet lag. I offer.

It started in Munich.

Now you've always been a little dreamy, but this new condition may be cause for some concern. I'm not saying you're heading for a tinfoil hat and sidewalk conversations with people who aren't there, but you never know how these things begin.

I think for a minute and then it dawns on me. *Munich, not Vienna?*

I know what you're thinking. But I don't know. Maybe it had to settle in. Maybe my cells had to rearrange. Truthfully, I'm not sure I'm not making it up.

What's it feel like?

It's the oddest thing I've ever experienced. It's like dreaming while being awake. Living in two different dimensions. It'd be maddening if I weren't so fascinated by it.

Sounds like the perfect affliction for a poet.

Well, there's that. It's also the kind of thing they lock people up for.

Don't be melodramatic.

WORDS: STUDY 7

words nap
on warm laundry.
words write poems

about sheets
hanging to dry.
words break free
from the clothesline
to float across the lawn.
words tumble into place.

words rest along the fenceline
and tangle with the grape vines.
words scatter over the yard,
gather under trees,
collect in the gutter.
words cling to the rake.

words stack themselves
into mountains of colors.
until we come

crashing into them
with our childlike pounces.
words break our fall.

PHILLIP

Sometimes words come easy. For you, apparently this isn't one of those times.

I don't understand how the same mind can be unfettered one day and bound like Prometheus the next. You complain.

It's early Sunday morning and I'm at *rembrandt* crafting a batch of croissants. On Sundays I'm usually pajama-clad and immersed in the *Times* at my kitchen table about now, not apron-clad and elbow-deep in dough. But the pastry chef is out this week. And making croissants is actually a religious experience for me.

Everyone says write what you know. But I'm just a waiter. All I know is eating and drinking.

Somehow I coaxed you into helping me today. I'd love to think it's my charm that sealed your fate, but I know that any excuse to avoid the white page on your computer is a good one.

Then write about the sensual world. There's an endless amount of material there. I lay out a fresh sheet of parchment paper on a cookie tray and spread the butter and flour mixture over its surface. Then I carry the tray to the reach-in and trade it for one that's already there.

I'm thinking of getting one of those books on writing, you say, as I stop what I'm doing to show you again how to knead the dough that's sitting in still life in front of you.

I say fuck what the books about writing say. They sell formulas, it's like a recipe you have to follow. I think it kind of kills the magic. Writing is kind of like alchemy, just like good cooking. I never measure anything. I kind of let the ingredients tell me what and how much. You have to step into the flow. Let the words take you where they want you to go. Don't try to control the process. I take the milk off the burner just before it scalds and stir in a little sugar and salt. Then I set this aside to cool.

Well, there is something other worldly about a nice meal or a good buzz. But I'm not sure I can stretch that into a novel.

Okay, then instead of trying to figure out what to write about, why don't you ask yourself what's keeping you from writing? I check the temperature of the milk with my finger and decide to wait. I spread a pastry cloth over one end of the butcher-block island and sprinkle it with flour. I lift the refrigerated dough from the cold tray and set it in the middle of the cloth.

Then it is definitely time. You know how I'm constantly concerned about time. About wasting it. About running out of it. About using it unwisely. To the point where it paralyzes me. And then I chase whatever distraction I can to avoid the issue.

I point for you to put the water on.

196

I think about this for a minute while I begin to roll the dough into a larger rectangle. *So, you're distracted by the fear of distraction?*

Don't make fun. Can't you see I'm in bad shape? But yes, that's exactly it. I have days and evenings that are set aside just for writing, but it seems those are the very days I can't seem to stick any words to the paper. And then the idea of the clock ticking away in the background just shuts down any creative idea I might have.

I put the butter in the center of the tray and wrap the dough around it, pinching the edges so it can't get out. *This way, I* explain to no one in particular, *it will have no choice but to saturate away any healthy thought the dough might have had of becoming a sensible pastry.*

I cover the dough and put it in the fridge, then turn back to you. *You are just going to hate what I'm about to say, but I'm going to say it anyway: I think you're trying too hard.*

I can see you are dumbfounded at the very idea of these words, because no one has ever accused you of that. You set down the wad of dough you've been mindlessly working.

You need to turn and look the monster in the face, Phillip. Stop running from it. Stop trying to beat time at its own game. Why not write a story about it, instead? Try to make time sexy, maybe. Seduce it right onto the page.

I check the milk again and decide it's cool enough. I take the water off the burner and add yeast, sprinkling it into the liquid without touching a measuring spoon, stirring as I go.

Make time sexy? Now there's a challenge. She's always been more like a jealous bitch. You sound incredulous, but I can tell I've tripped something.

Whatever works. I add the lukewarm milk mixture to the water, along with three coffee cups of flour, and go to work at blurring the lines between all the ingredients.

I'm so obsessed with this book right now, I can't even summon up a decent fantasy about whats-her-name...

Oh, so it isn't just the clock. Phillip, this is not the time to give up on that one. I told you before, she's your muse. If you can't find it in you to make time sexy, then at least write something about the thrill of the chase. But tell it from inside that girl's head.

You reach for your notebook.

Maybe the clock is telling you it's time to let go. Let your mind wander. Just like you do when you're reading a book. You've taken something that is supposed to bring you joy and made it work. You need to drop the discipline routine and foster a mindset of indulgence. The true mysteries of life lie in the sensual. And in the excess. It's not very interesting to deprive yourself of things, to make your life feel like a cardboard box. And you are not going to entice any words to the page that way, either.

I scoop the soft new dough out of the bowl and onto a different pastry cloth. I go to work on it with my fingers and the palms of my hands.

So all the eating and drinking and pursuing women I've done has just been training, research for this story? And rather than curtail that mindset, I should indulge in it to feed my muse?

I finish smoothing the dough, cover it and set it on top of the oven to rise.

Careful, I might get the impression that you're listening to me.

I return to the reach-in and pull out a third tray of dough. I flour the first cloth again and cut the dough into 4 equal pieces. I set three of them aside and roll the one remaining into a circle about the size of a small pizza. Then I take a rounded blade and cut the dough into 6 slices, as if it were a pizza.

I am listening. Which shows how desperate I am. You grin, but you've stopped pretending like you're helping me and are just sitting on a stool with your buttery, floury hands in your lap.

A celebration of the senses will always have a place at literature's table, because it gives people permission to be human. Imaginary sensual experiences are almost as good as the real thing. Sometimes better.

I pick up a slice of dough, placing the wide end closest to me. And then I roll the dough away from my stomach until I come to the pointed end.

So the things that have distracted me from writing all this time are actually the things I need to tell my story. Who would've guessed.

I bend the dough to look like a crescent moon and then brush it with a frothy combination of egg yolks and milk.

Life's a paradox. Now, if you're not going to do anything but sit there, then go play with your new word friends. I reach for another slice.

REMBRANDT: STUDY 4

the painter had no need for sun.
he watched as a child
and saw the world

already filled with light.
all things breathed it
like radiant oxygen.
it came not from a single source,
was neither this color nor that.
he saw the light

needed the dark.
each held the other.
neither slept.

MAGGIE

Going to jail is a frightening thing. Even if you're just there for a visit. There are psychologists who say that deep down, we're all criminals. It's in the collective unconscious, in our DNA, in our muscle memory. Maybe this explains why every time you have to empty your pockets, leave your bar card with the authorities, and pass through the metal scanners, the thought is there.

Nobody wants to get caught on the wrong side of a criminal indictment. Innocent until proven guilty is crap. If that's true why are people put in jail until they're proven innocent? People read in the paper about an arrest for a crime and silently they have already condemned that person. The system is set up to convict. So no matter how irrational the fear, most people cringe walking into a cage.

As you traverse the sterile corridors following the color-coded stripes on the floor, you think again how sick a decision it was to mark this route with black tape. With each heavy metal door that closes behind you, you feel a twinge of helplessness, like Algernon the mouse on a bad day.

When the last electromagnetic lock clanks behind you, you welcome the chance to be in the large visiting room.

A series of bulletproof windows to the right shield guards who speak to you through an intercom. The walls are painted industrial shades of green, there are high ceilings, and the lights are clinically bright. In your opinion, the bright lights sort of defeat the purpose of the psychologically calm paint, but no one asked you. There are vending machines and a microwave along one wall. In the middle of the floor sit several long tables neatly arranged in rows. All the chairs are the same. Blue plastic with chrome legs. Everything is visible from the guard's station.

Straight ahead, there are four normal looking doors with large windows leading to attorney interview rooms. Perforated tiles on the walls in these rooms give the appearance of secrecy, but that's all it is, appearance. You have to talk about strategy and the facts of the case sometime though—and you know the phones aren't safe—so you do what you can. Sometimes you write on paper, sometimes you whisper. Sometimes you wad up scratch paper while you talk.

It might seem like other fears would come from being sealed in a room with death row inmates, especially since the prison authorities find it necessary to put the guards behind bulletproof glass. But you are more afraid of the guards locking you in than you are of being injured by an inmate.

You sit down in one of the interview rooms. You pull out a draft of a letter to the Tribal Chairman you've been working on and go over it as you wait for the guards to bring in Mercado. When they bring him in, he is in full shackles. You order them removed, nodding to the guard that you will accept the safety risk. You place your hand lightly on his shoulder as they unlock the metal cuffs. He takes a seat across the table from you and the guard shuts the door.

He looks tired. Dark circles under his eyes and a paleness you never see anywhere but prison. His native skin is normally darker than yours. It's as if his skin surrendered its pigment along with its freedom. Checked it at the booking area along with personal items. If he went before a jury today, they'd surely convict him all over again. He has the zombie look of someone who works in a basement all day, fluorescent lights his only sun. Everything about his environment is artificial. False lights. False air. False food. Surreal is a word that doesn't do it justice. It's better than Kafka could've written it.

You begin making some small talk to relax him. You lie and tell him that he looks good. At first you feel like you are talking to an empty shell. You become concerned he has snapped, disappeared somewhere inside. You've seen it happen. In fact, you are more surprised when it doesn't.

As you talk, gradually Steve Mercado begins to emerge. His voice becomes stronger and his spark begins to reappear. You go through the high points of the briefs, your notes for oral arguments, the questions the justices may ask. You tell him things you've told him before. There's always a chance the state supreme court will grant the appeal, but relief most likely lies in the hands of higher federal courts. You never promise him anything. It's better to let him get by on his own reserves than to give him false hope. There are enough false things here.

You explain again there is no way to know when the court will issue an opinion. Could be a month, could be a year. Mercado nods to tell you he understands. But you know you'll have to answer this question any number of times before the opinion is finally handed down.

Most clients in here are so desperate to change their circumstances that they create an elaborate new reality for themselves. And they become like drunks, telling you the same things over and over again. Asking the same questions. Posing the same conspiracy theories. But Mercado is different, he has a different sort of calm. He has done well, you think. He has gone inside, but hasn't let this place take away what's him, not yet.

He spots the letter you're working on and asks about it. This is his pattern with you, he's always trying to connect to some piece of the world outside his unchanging microcosm. In his letters to you he commonly asks questions about your life. It's understandable that he wants to hear stories of someone driving to work, eating in a restaurant, watching rented movies with friends, having cold beer and buttered popcorn. Normally you do your best to keep your personal life separate from this world. But occasionally you crack the door and let someone have a peek.

Are you writing to the tribe about my case? He asks.

No, it's just another case I've been working on. You answer.

You probably can't talk about it, huh?

You open your mouth again, but nothing comes out.

You change the subject and ask about his little brother, if he is staying out of trouble. You tell Mercado to have him call if he ever needs any help. You ask if he is getting any exercise. He says he does plenty of push-ups and sit ups everyday, but their yard time is limited.

You make more small talk, mostly aimed at getting Mercado to talk, so he will remember his voice. Then it's time for you to go. You can tell he is growing anxious about having to sink back inside and become made of lead again. You pull a paperback copy of *The Meadow* out of your bag and slide it across the table. Never much of a reader in the outside world, Mercado has taken it up since he's been inside. It helps him escape his reality and fill up the hours in the day that are otherwise spent staring at four tight walls.

It's already been cleared. You add. With that you rise from your chair, shake his hand, and gather up your things.

He thanks you and tells you to go to a baseball game for him. The guard begins putting the manacles back on him. Then, as you wait for the heavy buzzer and the hydraulic door to open so you can begin your long trek though the sterile labyrinth towards freedom, the guard waits to lead Steve Mercado out a side door. But he has already disappeared somewhere else.

LOVE: STUDY 7

love likes strong coffee.
love spoons fresh cream.
love is drizzled in honey.

love steams your glasses
when you take it
to your lips.

love goes down smooth.
love warms your hands.
love speeds your heart.

love is liquid adrenaline.
love is mango ice cream.
eaten with a wooden spoon.

melting on your tongue.
love is a cancer.
waiting to consume you.

DILLON

Did you ever see any lions in Africa? You ask.

I'm stirring up a batch of peanut butter and chocolate chip cookies. I look up.

Sure.

Really?

Yeah. They were near the property sometimes. But they tend to stay away from people. Why? I push a strand of hair out of my eyes with the one wrist not covered in flour.

I don't think I've ever seen a real lion. You confess.

I cock my head. I'm not sure why I think this is odd. Just something I take for granted maybe, that everyone has seen a lion. *Of course you've seen a lion, somewhere.*

I mean, you know, that wasn't shot full of Depakote and laying around in a big cage. You lean over the bowl and run your index finger along the inside edge, reminding me where most people actually see what were once lions.

Well, you know the saying. If you see one in the wild, it'll likely be the last thing. I warn.

Unless... You put your finger in your mouth, slowly retracting it.

I stop and sample the goods as well. When you don't finish your thought, I add: *Okay, I'll play. Unless what?*

Unless you are a lion, you say, revealing your still-dough-sullied digit and a quizzical grin.

Whatever that means. I say, scraping batter off my own finger with my teeth, wondering half-heartedly where this is going.

You get up and walk over to the fireplace. You look around like you're thinking about stirring coals, looking for a fireplace tool. Problem is, there's no fire going.

I watch you fidget for a while, nervously half-pacing, starting to sit, looking for something to put your hands on. You turn from the fireplace to the balcony. You stare out the French doors into the clouds that have descended from their posts in the sky to crawl along the foothills.

Are you okay? I finally ask, after realizing I'm uncomfortable for you.

What do you mean? You ask, as if you're not acting like you are barely attached to the planet.

I mean, different than your usual not-quite okay? I pull out a long sheet of wax paper and tear it off with the metal teeth glued to the edge of the box. I lay it on top of a cookie sheet I've set on the counter.

I mean, since I've been back, my sense of reality has been a little out-of-whack. Your back is still to me.

How do you mean? I mean, how is it compared to your usual sense of reality? It is a legitimate question.

I'm talking mostly about the part where I feel like I'm dreaming while I'm awake. And awake while I'm asleep. You explain, sort of.

Ok, what's this got to do with lions? Are there lions on my deck? Are you imagining there are? I can't hide the incredulous tone of my voice. In a belated attempt to mask it, I return to stirring.

Well, no. Not right now. That's probably because of the black bear, though. You've located an iron poker and start to play with a fire that hasn't been built. I stop stirring again.

That's a local. He's just looking for scraps. He'll make his way to the dumpster sooner or later. So do you see these lions while you're awake or asleep? I take a spoon from a drawer and scoop out a ball of dough. I slide the dough from the spoon with my fingers and roll it between my palms. Then I place it on one corner of the wax paper.

I'm not sure. But I think I'm asleep. You say earnestly.

Are you going to make me keep fishing here without any bait? I reach back into the bowl with the spoon for another ball of dough.

If I tell you, you promise not to laugh? You set the poker aside and finally look straight at me.

No. But tell me anyway. I press the dough with my fingers, molding it into another lumpy, shiny, delicious ball of unbaked heaven.

I think I am a lion.

I don't flinch.

You mean you were a lion, like in another life or something? I place the new ball on the wax paper.

You don't exactly answer. It's more like half a shrug.

Well, I mean, we probably both were, don't you think. I mean, don't you think we've been everything? I continue with my process, pretending I'm some sort of clay artist, sculpting tiny raw pieces of art.

Maybe. You shrug. You poke at the imaginary fire again, turn over a log that isn't there.

You can't just stop there. I drop the spoon in the bowl.

You know how every now and then you have a dream that's so real you can't tell the difference? I mean usually something in you knows you're dreaming. But sometimes you have a dream that is so vivid, you're baffled when you wake up and find it isn't true.

Yeah. I know that. Is all I say.

Okay, here's the weird part. It feels perfectly normal to be this lion.

And foreign to be human when you wake up. I say. But there are many other things I don't say. I don't, for instance, explain how I know this. I don't say, *Yeah, I've had that exact same dream.* Because really, who would believe that. Not even you would believe I wasn't just stealing thunder.

Yes. Exactly. You don't ask, thankfully. Your affliction provides welcome distraction. I decide I can fit more cookies on this sheet, so I pick up the spoon again. Do people really have the exact same dream? Does the collective unconscious really go that deep?

We're both quiet for a minute. I realize I forgot to turn on the oven.

It costs a lot of money to go on Safari. I say, reaching up on my shelves for the jar of sugar.

I'm sure. You pause, then look puzzled. *Why would you say that?*

Aren't you planning your next escape already? I have to stand on my tiptoes to bring down the jar.

I haven't gotten that far.

How far have you gotten? I open the jar and place it on the counter next to the cookie sheet.

Actually, I'm thinking about going to India, next.

Dillon, you're not becoming a seeker are you? I mean, India? That's a little bit cliché isn't it? I don't know why I've turned against you on this.

That's an odd thing to come out of your mouth. You stop playing with imaginary fire again. You come back to the kitchen and sit at the bar.

I mean, I've dreamt of lions, but I'm not going to go traipsing across the globe looking for them just because they popped up in a dream. I dip a fork in the sugar and flatten one of the little balls of dough.

Yeah, but you've already seen them. You pick up one of the pre-squashed balls of peanut butter and chocolate and pop it whole into your mouth. I shoot you a look, but the look says I wish I would've done that first, more than it says you're in trouble.

True. I say, forming a smaller ball and putting it into my own mouth before it even sees the wax paper.

It's not like I dreamed I was naked at school. You manage somehow with a mouth full of raw cookie.

Interesting analogy. I move the cookie sheet out of your grasp so at least a few of these babies will find their way to the oven.

WORDS: STUDY 8

words are not human.
you can eat a word.
you can kill a word.

you can starve a word to death.
words will always come back.
words are powerful.

words fail.
words remind you
of someone you know.

words don't care
whether you hear them
if they fall in the forest.

PHILLIP

Once there was a boy named *time*. He grew up like most kids, meandering, playing ball, chasing cats, eating his vegetables. He learned by exploring the things around him, came to know himself in relation to these things. He paid little attention to grown ups and their efforts to build fences for him, schedule their lives around him.

Like most boys, he was more concerned with expanding his world than obeying its limits. Lost in a land of *let's pretend*, he created rolling horizons without borders and universes without boundaries. His mind was focused on the task at hand, not what would come next. When lunch was ready, he would be called. When darkness fell, he would go inside. He assumed this was the way his world would be forever.

As happens, eventually he began to go through changes. He started to feel new things, to see himself and the things around him differently. He moved more swiftly, became hungrier, noticed girls. The world was shiny and new. He visited new neighborhoods, tried new food, stayed up late. He didn't want to miss anything.

Again, he thought life would be this way forever.

And then one day he woke up. On his way to the kitchen for a cup of coffee, he passed a clock in the hallway. He stopped to look at himself in its glass and accidentally got a new glimpse of who he was. He panicked. He began to fall apart. Slowly at first, then rapidly. Nothing was as it seemed. It was as if overnight, the world he knew was stolen and replaced with one that looked the same, but wasn't. It was as if someone had let him in on a lifelong secret, an unpleasant truth he'd been sheltered from his whole life. He would never be the same.

How could he have lived so carelessly for so long? How was he so blind to his own nature? And how did it come to pass that so many people depended upon him, scheduled their lives around his own, worshiped his name? Worse yet, for everyone who revered him, there was another who cursed his name, spat at the idea of him.

The most uncomfortable thing was the realization that there was nothing he could do. No matter what, his life would march forward. There was no stopping, no getting off the ride. No matter how he tried. He would get drunk, stay out all night, and sometimes sleep for days. Still he would keep moving. When he awoke, slowly he'd realize that he hadn't changed a thing. That his namesake marched on, even in his sleep. He was unstoppable. He could not be incarcerated, distracted, or derailed.

He tried everything, including seduction. But even in the arms of beauty, he was not paralyzed. He consulted holy men, great thinkers, prostitutes. But no one seemed to have the answer to his riddle.

Years passed. Then one day, while walking across an old stone bridge, he saw a glimpse of freedom. A woman stood on one side, her head bowed, sobbing quietly, tears streaming down her face. He watched her as she looked down at the river flowing quickly beneath her feet. He wanted to comfort her, but had no idea what he could ever do that would make her feel better. Then, as if she suddenly became inspired, she lifted her head, removed her wedding ring and tossed it bravely into the water.

Apparently gratified by the act, she continued. Next came her diamond earrings, then a bracelet, followed by another ring. Finally, she unfastened her watch and flung it too into the rapids below. As the watch came to rest in the river bottom, the young man instantly felt a small relief.

The secret, he realized, was that he only existed in people's minds. He was their creation. Just like the watch. A metaphor. A line on a two-dimensional plane. An oversimplified way for them to measure their lives.

If he could just get people to stop thinking about him, he could disappear. He could escape the cages they'd built for him. But how was this possible? Everywhere there were timepieces painstakingly constructed in his name. How had this cult grown so large? How had they become so dependent upon him? How had they mistaken the tree for the fruit?

He went immediately to the nearest clock he could find and punched it square in the nose. The big hand lost its place first and both soon fell slack into six thirty. He started breaking into jewelry stores and clock repair shops, smashing the wristwatches and pulling the guts from grandfather clocks. In public places and in broad daylight, he couldn't pass a clock without moving time forward and backward. He snickered to himself as he watched people take morning lunches and have after-work cocktails in the noonday sun. They would show up at work when the day was nearly over and puzzle over why the sun was still up at bedtime.

While these mischievous acts always made him feel better, he realized eventually that he would never fix the problem on his own. So he devised a plan. Late one night while a young writer was sleeping, he crept in his open window and scribbled a few lines on a scratch pad.

So now, if you know what's good for you, if you have a heart and are willing to be brave, do us all a favor. Break your clocks. Smash your watches. Free time.

LOVE: STUDY 8

love spills ink on the page
and asks what you see.
love crayons your walls

and fingerpaints your bookshelves.
love uses your notes for kindling.
love pastes stickers on your calendar.
love erases your speed dial.
love draws pictures on your resume
and ties your hands with your belts.

MAGGIE

Some days are diamonds. Some are coal. Grimy, dirty, sooty, greasy, stinky coal. This is one of those days for you. A coal day. And you find yourself without a lantern or headgear.

On your way back from the computer store, after having spent half your morning in technology hell over a crashed laptop, you stop in the café to have a cup of coffee and rant about the state of the modern world.

What happened to the idea of service, Jillian? You ask as you climb onto a barstool.

What, I've got ESP? You just sat down. I put up my hands.

I mean in general. What has happened? From car dealers to computer makers, nobody is willing to take responsibility anymore. You put your hands in your long hair and pull from both sides.

I hold up a pot. *Joe?*

Yeah. Better throw in something to make it interesting though. You nod to the shelves.

I think it started with politics. I pour a cup of coffee. *Then it just caught on.* I follow with a shot of Tuaca.

Well, it used to be financially smart to treat customers well. You know, word-of-mouth, repeat business, building a reputation. What happened? You take a sip, nod in approval.

I think it's called amnesia. I light a cigarette and blow a stream of smoke straight up.

I didn't know you smoked? You set down the cup.

I don't. I say with a straight face. *Someone left these on the bar last night.*

What's amnesia got to do with it? You slide the pack across the bar, tilt the end and tap one out.

Somewhere big-business figured out that the American public has amnesia. Basically, we're too busy to remember to hold a grudge. Look at Wal-Mart. They dismantled the retail industry in this country from one end to the other and yet, at any given time, you can drive by and the parking lot is chock-full. Why is it when you come in to talk I end up ranting too?

Maybe that's it. We've all just given up. You pick up the cigarette and tap the filtered end on the bar while you drink your coffee.

Maybe we all just think someone else will pick up the sword. I know the modern world can't exactly be summed up this easily. In some ways we have it better than any generation in history. But it isn't exactly uncomplicated either. And people seem to be crumpling under the weight of daily stress far more than they used to.

Let me tell you from experience, the fucking sword gets heavy. You lean back and, with longer motions, exaggerate the tap of the cigarette on the bar.

I pick up a book of matches and lean forward. *How about a light?*

Back at your office, you are setting up your new computer. When it's done, you sort through the mail, filing and throwing away. There is the usual junk, sales pitches and credit card offers. And the necessary evils, bank statements and credit card bills, copies of court dockets and notices of property taxes.

There is also a noticeably thick envelope from the state supreme court. You pick it up, hesitantly eager. It could be a decision on any of a number of appeals. But somehow you know it isn't. It's the Mercado decision. You hadn't expected it so soon. But that's what it has to be. You hold it in one hand and pull the letter opener across the top with the other. Then you slide the folded bundle from its package, open the pages, and crease the folds backwards. Your eyes check the caption to be sure: *Steve Mercado vs. State.* You don't take time to read the court's introductory synopsis, but quickly scan down to the last word in the syllabus: AFFIRMED.

Your heart sinks. You put down the bundle of papers. Stare out the window. *Gutless bastards!* You aren't sure why you react this way. You weren't under any illusion that they had the courage to grant relief on the case. Perhaps you were secretly hoping for a miracle. In truth, you have far more faith in people than you let on. You have to be an interminable optimist to work on death penalty cases. It's like being a Cubs fan.

You still believe his case will ultimately be overturned on federal appeal, but that's a long time for Mercado to wait. A long time for his spirit to have to hide, for it to risk extermination. A long time for him to be tempted by the urge to *volunteer*, to give up the appeal process and allow the State to proceed with the execution.

In all likelihood, the court will appoint someone else to take the federal case. If you are completely honest, you are disappointed in part because you want to be the one. You want to be Steve Mercado's personal savior.

You give a long sigh, pick up the decision again and begin to read the court's conjured reasoning. You make notes in the margins. Then, before you finish reading, you do something you aren't sure you'll get away with. You call the prison and ask for a deputy warden who has pulled strings for you in the past. You ask him in the most charming voice you can muster if it's possible for him to bring Mercado to the phone. Though it is unorthodox, the way you asked him, he can either go get the prisoner or admit he doesn't have that kind of authority.

The warden puts you on hold as he radios the unit. As it happens, Mercado is being relayed back to his section from a visit to the infirmary. The warden comes back on the line and tells you if he can catch Mercado before count, he can route him to a phone. He tells you to wait. He walkie-talkies then to Mercado's escort and redirects him to a phone bank. The next voice you hear is Mercado's.

Hello?

Hey Steve. It's Maggie. I'm going to file the federal habeas. You don't waste time.

They shot us down, huh? Mercado doesn't sound surprised.

Yeah. Look, I'm really sorry. You hate giving him the news like this, but you think the sooner the better. Fast and quick, like pulling off a band-aid.

I'll tell you a secret. I never thought we'd get anywhere with those state judges. They gotta be re-elected. I just didn't wanna take the wind outta your sails. Mercado is calm. *I'm glad they came down so early. Now we can get it on with the feds.*

You know, we may be spending too much time together, you're starting to sound like me. I'll file the federal forms next week. You can't tell him that the federal court will probably appoint someone else. You'll make another trip down later for that. You say goodbye, hang up, and place the decision back on your desk.

It's one thirty. You head back to the café. The lunch crowd is clearing out by the time you get there. You sit down at the bar and order a pilsner. While I clean up and restock, you sip the beer and pick up our conversation from this morning. You tell me the news about Mercado.

Do you ever think that all the shit that happens in our lives is there for a reason? You run your middle finger around the rim of the glass. For an instant you look uncharacteristically helpless. Like a young girl on the side of the road with a flat tire and no idea how to use the jack.

What, the whole idea of destiny? I ask. *I gotta tell you, if that's the way things are, it kinda pisses me off.* I pour myself half a beer and sit down across the bar from you.

Right, like what's the point. You take a deep drink of your beer. When you look up, your eyes are clouded. You reach for the pack of cigarettes still on the bar and shake one loose.

I strike a match for you, then I light my own. But I hesitate before speaking, staring at the counter, blowing smoke onto the bar. *There's a saying that the strings of a lute don't know their own music until they're strummed.* I look up at you, then back at my beer. You pull on your cigarette. There is a long pause where we both avoid eye contact, smoking and tapping our ashes in the ashtray.

Why do we have such poor memory of sound? You finally ask, your voice thick.

You mean amnesia? I ask, blowing out more smoke, trying to lighten things up.

Ah, we've come full circle. You smile a little.

Because we're an arrogant breed. The complacency is bad enough. If we had better memories, we'd convince ourselves there was nothing more to know and we'd just quit trying altogether. I take a final drag and crush my cigarette out in the ashtray.

Point taken. You tilt your glass.

That's our lot, they say. To be given paradise with no way to hold it. I lift my own glass to meet yours.

⎯⎯

You're not gone 45 minutes when you sit back down in front of me, toss an envelope on the bar, and order another pilsner.

Apparently, when you returned to your office again, you picked up the rest of the mail you had put aside to read the Mercado decision. Tucked conspiratorially in the middle of the stack was an envelope from the Sowha tribe.

Looks like three's the magic number today. You say, as I slide the beer into your open palm.

I pick up the envelope and remove its contents. I unfold the pages, but before I can get past the first sentence, you begin to explain. The letter contains a Notice to Vacate. It gives the café 60 days to wrap things up. Virgil has already told me that if this is the tribe's position, he's not going to fight it. He remains willing to battle the Government, but says it isn't a good idea to prepare food in a house where you've become an unwelcome guest.

Well, good news is the triangle's complete. You can relax now. I put the letter down and slide it and the envelope back in your direction.

Stupid thing is, I'm feeling sorry for myself instead of for Virgil and Grace. You consider the top of your beer for a minute. *I'm an asshole.* You say, finally laughing.

Secretly, I believe Virgil and Grace have grown a little restless and wouldn't be heartbroken to have an excuse to seek out a new adventure. I think having me around to run the café has allowed them to consider what else they want to do.

There's still a few smokes in the pack, so I fish one out, light it, and hand it to you. You accept it without hesitation, pulling an ashtray closer and tapping the cigarette on the rim before taking a deep drag. You hold your breath for a few seconds, then blow a hearty stream of smoke into the air. You laugh again, almost in spite of yourself, and ask me, *What am I doing?*

Well, right now you're drinking German beer and smoking a French cigarette.

I mean with my life. You sigh.

I could tell you. But then, as the Buddhists say, I'd have to kill you.

I reach over and lift the cigarette from between your fingers, then put it to my lips. *I forgot how goddamn good these things are.* I say, holding it up to the light.

LOVE: STUDY 9

love is not a self-help book.
love is not a weekend seminar.
love is a list you throw away.

love is not a guru.
love won't charge you for answers.
love doesn't swim with dolphins.

love doesn't swim with sharks.
love swims naked in the moonlight.
love pulls you into the water.

DILLON

Y ou awake again in Timbavati. But this time you are not sleeping, not waking from slumber. You are crouched in the tall grass, electricity charging through your every nerve. If you were any more alert, you'd wake your dead ancestors.

In the desert, it has been said, you can remember your name. But a name doesn't have to be a word. And you haven't time to think about this now. Your gaze is fixed, unmovable.

Throughout history, lions have depicted royalty. Legend tells of the moon goddess who was in charge of time. She marked the seasons and had the power to speed up, slow down, and suspend the movement of time. She seduced the seas to rise at her beckon, the rivers to swell in their flow, and the wolves to sing her operas at night.

Unlike the sun god, she was able to move in the darkness as well as the light. The sun god was jealous of this power. So the moon goddess mostly stayed away from him, continually reinventing herself as a disguise.

It was said that the sun—intrigued by the moon's mystery—had once been her suitor and had pursued her with a tenacity that was quite extraordinary, even for the gods. But the sun could only move through the day, and moon could not be confined to walking in only half the world. Because the sun was a jealous god, he attempted to lock up the moon goddess in a tower atop the mountain of the gods, beside the Sea of Eternity. In this way, he thought, she would always be with him.

The moon goddess was both hurt and outraged. She couldn't believe the sun god did not understand that her loyalty to him depended not upon the season of the days, but was eternal, like the lines of a circle. From her window, she looked out at the sea and summoned her twin who lived in the water. Together they gathered the wild sea horses and set them in motion. The force of the stampede lifted waves high enough to bring the horses crashing into the stones of the castle, dismantling it forever and releasing the moon goddess and her lover into the night.

After that, the moon goddess changed her appearance once more. Since she walked both in the darkness and in the light, she understood the circular wholeness of the universe. She knew she could never truly lose a part of herself there, so she devised a plan to spread out her powers. She set about diffusing her essence throughout the world, so that if the sun did decide to renew his efforts, he would never be able to capture all of her again.

She placed these pieces of herself in the most difficult of places: the tops of mountains, the sources of rivers, caves beneath the sea. And she chose two great lions to carry the last two pieces with them.

Since the time of the original gift, these lions and their descendants walk mostly at night, when the moon is most visible. The moon goddess still remembers her days with the sun, before his jealousy overcame him. In homage to those days, as well as an offering of peace, from time to time she casts a shadow of herself in his presence. Likewise, the lions occasionally roam during the day, to give honor to the sun god, and to keep themselves in balance with the great circle.

⎯⎯

You know you can't outrun the striped pony. You are quick, far quicker than he, but he beats you on endurance. If he catches on that you are near, you're almost certain to fail.

You must use the old trick. You must make yourself invisible.

You wake with a jolt, your sheets wet, your heart racing, the taste of blood in your mouth. As soon as you can catch your breath, you reach for your phone and dial my number.

WORDS: STUDY 9

words are a mystery.
words leave few clues.
words meet in dark alleys.

and plan conspiracies.
words hide their weapons.
words have connections.
words shapeshift
into other shapes
and blend into crowds.

words wear black.
words dance in carnival.
love is a word.

love is the word.
love writes its own story.
love writes you in.

PHILLIP

You awake today with a sense of panic. You decide to sit down and write through it, but you need a little liquid encouragement. You go to your cupboard, but as soon as you open the door, you remember there are no coffee beans. You scraped the bottom of the ceramic container yesterday. It sits beside the sink with its open mouth mocking you and your condition, its dangling latch sticking its tongue out at you.

The café's still closed. You come through the back door and nod almost imperceptibly as you pass me and head straight behind the bar. You stop at the espresso machine and reach beside it to flip the switches, but I'm way ahead of you.

It's already warm. I say, at the same time you spot my cup sitting on the bar.

Cool. Is all you say.

Help yourself. I don't mask the sarcasm.

When you finally sit down, double shot in hand, arms splayed and body contorted in your signature pose, you look at me with a surprising manner of desperation and say, *What if I can't do it? What if I can't figure it out?*

Love, you mean, but I don't get that right away.

I read your piece about time, Phillip. If you ask me, you've got it. You just need to run with it.

No, not writing. Well, okay, that too. But I mean, after the chase. I know what'll happen, Jill. She'll start to get comfortable and I'll start to feel suffocated.

What brought on this fit of consciousness? I ask, as I take an extra-large mixing bowl from behind the bar.

I had this amazing dream last night.

Yeah, what about?

That's just it. I can't fucking remember.

I break open a gallon of milk and pour it into the bowl. Then I add a quart of heavy cream and stir just a little.

I'm confused. Then how do you know it was amazing?

Well, I just remember the feeling. But what occurred to me is, that having the dream is not that incredible. Remembering it. Hanging on to it. That's the hard part. And I started thinking, getting the girl, that's not the hard part. It's keeping the girl. Hanging onto whatever it is. That's the trick.

Funny the blur between that world and this one. How dreams slip through our fingers like water when crossing the border. As if in that world, we can hold water in our open hands without any problem, and we continually forget that it's impossible in this world.

And then, before I can even get out of bed, it hits me.

What does?

It's just the same with writing. It's like there's this dream world where all these secrets are kept and where all the good writing lives. But there's a border patrol army that protects everything there. It's their job to see that these things aren't leaked out into the waking world. They'll let you come and go freely enough, but you have to smuggle these things out if you want them. And you have to be really fucking good to get away with it.

I open a carton of eggs and begin cracking, pouring, and separating into two smaller bowls.

What happened today? You weren't able to carry the dream over the border?

Must've got caught on the fence. I think I had to ditch most of what I was carrying, so I could get away.

I add a cup (or so) of sugar to the egg yolks and start to work them together.

You're worried, then, because even though the writing is going well right now, you're afraid that sooner or later you're going to get caught by the border patrol.

I push the bowl with the egg whites towards you and hand you a whisk.

Bingo. You say, staring for a minute at the implement in your hand.

Come on, what are they going to do to you if they catch you? Whether you're in the middle of a dream or not, look the monster in the face. Tell the border patrol to fuck off and take what you want.

You don't respond. Instead, you look down at the bowl in front of you and go to work like you're fusing subatomic particles.

I scan the shelves and take down a single-barrel bourbon. *Somehow, you finally decided you had a right to the ideas, and then they started coming.*

I took your advice and looked the time-monster in the face. You know it pains me to say it, but you were right, by making time one of my characters, it's now at my mercy, instead of the other way around.

Ok, how's this all relate to your crimson muse? I decide to tie up the strings, as I slowly stir the bourbon into the egg yolks. You've finished with the whites, so I take a pure cane rum from the shelves and with a small spatula gently add it to the egg whites.

God forbid it's true, but what if I have changed? What if—for some unforeseen reason—I don't want to set her up for failure? Even if I can hold onto dreams and great ideas from the underworld,

I'm not sure I can hold on to my feelings for her. You look a bit forlorn, as if this answer has authentically pained you.

Why not let her off the hook, then? I say, as I lift the yolk whiskey and drizzle it into to the egg white rum.

Just like that? Aren't you going to tell me not to give up, that if I figure her out, I'll figure my writing out?

No. I don't look up. I'm busy marrying the boozy egg soup into the milk and cream.

Why not? You sound like an actor whose co-star has deviated from the script.

I continue mixing, but I look up long enough to catch your eye. *Because you're there. You don't need a muse anymore. And because I want to encourage this sudden fit of compassion you're having, even if you had to steal it from the dreamworld.*

You're silent.

I consider the shelves again and my eyes land on a French brandy. Using a fine strainer, I add this, too, to my concoction, taking care not to let it touch the bottom of the bowl before it's folded into the froth. *You're not the same person you were six months ago. You are re-creating yourself as you re-create your novel.* I explain, actually a little concerned about your paucity of words.

Still no sound from you. I rinse one of the egg bowls and dry it, along with the whisk. I open a second quart of heavy cream and pour part of it into the clean bowl. I add some Tahitian vanilla, pure maple syrup, and fresh nutmeg, and start to whisk these final ingredients.

When I'm finished, I take down two white wine glasses and a ladle. I fill each glass halfway and then top them with the whipped cream. I set one in front of you and raise the other one in the air.

Never hurts to get a solid jump on the holidays. You say, as you lift your glass to meet mine.

Here's to smugglers everywhere. I toast.

REMBRANDT: STUDY 5

the painter's back grew weak.
the words held him up.
he lost his money, his address,

his wives, his children, his position.
the words always knew
where to find him.

the painter was stripped
of society, comfort,
reputation.
the words came anyway.
they were unhindered,
unashamed.

the last of his years
beat him, left him
for dead.
the words
were never brighter,
never more sure of themselves.

the man suffered.
the artist was untouched,
thriving on stolen paint

and sleeping outside
to soak up more words.
the painter's story
cannot be told
by anyone else.
his words alone

explain everything.
until they crack and peel away,
no one will tell the story better.

MAGGIE

You know, people say the law is a jealous mistress. But that's not really true.

No?

No. It's more like an abusive spouse.

It's late on a Friday night. The dinner rush is over, but the *café's* still about half full. People are ordering coffee and lingering over their half-eaten desserts. Couples are still working on their bottles of wine, leaning closer to each other. Everyone is reluctant to leave and break the spell.

You look and sound like you're more than two fingers into the bottle of whiskey tonight. I slide a menu your way and pour you a glass of water. *Hungry?* I ask as I set the water in front of you.

No. But I should probably eat. You reluctantly admit.

I take a basket of bread and butter from behind the bar and set it between us. *Here, this is good for soaking up whatever we spill.*

I fold back the linen and start to butter a piece of bread for myself. I realize I'm famished. *The rush started before I could order myself dinner.* I explain, before hurrying the combination to my mouth.

I'm wondering how long it will be before you'll name the demon you've been wrestling tonight. Or if. But before I can finish swallowing my snack, you begin filling out the nametag.

On the road to enlightenment, there's a lot of madness, don't you think? We just seem so far away sometimes I'm not sure we're gonna make it.

Well, not with gas prices the way they are. I say, starting on another piece of bread. You don't laugh.

It's a big world, right? Of all the ways to make money, how did I end up in the law?

I butter another piece, but I hand this one to you, as you still haven't made any move towards the basket. You take it, but still make no effort to get it into your mouth.

This would be a good time for me to come up with an answer. But I've got nothing. I'm plenty compassionate, but I have more compassion for people like you who are willing to fight unpopular fights, than I do for your clients. Right now, though, I'm mostly focused on trying to change the future. Specifically, the part where you wake up feeling like you got hit by a train. At least you haven't started repeating yourself.

I'm sorry, I know I'm being tragic. You bite the side of your lip, instead of the bread, which you've set down on the plate. *It's like I've said before, I'm kind of masquerading. I don't think I have the stomach for this.* You unroll your silverware and fumble with your napkin before you place it in your lap.

Let me get you some real food. How about a bowl of gumbo? A little protein, a little rice? I ask as I'm simultaneously putting in the order. I'm also thinking that it's already made, so it'll be the shortest distance between the kitchen and your stomach. You shrug a little and nod.

It's like this light came on, and suddenly I can see through everyone, not just lawyers and judges, everyone. I see the lies they try to believe about why they do their jobs. I see their worn-out relationships. I can feel their loneliness, their desperation as they look around for an exit route. Lately, I can almost see their thoughts. I wonder how psychics stay sane.

Who says they are. Who says anyone is.

Look around in here. There are a few people who are still half-awake, trying to fight the sandman. But that's it. Almost everyone has come to accept a different kind of life than they ever imagined. I feel like an alien who just landed on earth and I'm looking around going, What the hell are you people doing?

I think it's safe to say we've gotten to the prime time show. Your temperature has gone up along with your volume. In the least condescending way I can manage, I smile while I gesture to the gallery and motion for you to keep it down a little. But I decide that the best way to keep you quiet until your food comes is to take the floor for a minute.

You're talking about the lie. I say, in a hushed voice as I lean closer to you.

What lie? You ask.

There's a lie out there that's so big it's hard to see around. I begin. *It's the responsibility lie. And it's sold in bulk by the haves. The lie has many faces. It can look like cars or clothes or any number of smart containers. But its primary message is: Give up your childhood dreams. Do it in the name of safety and security. Do it because it's time to grow up. Do it because these are the things you really want. Tangible goods. Not ephemeral dreams. The lie says that we all have to cross this threshold. That you are irresponsible if you don't. And of course, the hardest thing is that almost everyone is in on it. If you don't live in a cave somewhere, it's impossible to avoid.*

The gumbo arrives just in time. I set it in front of you and hand you a big spoon and some hot sauce. You finally seem interested in eating. You carelessly dash out the hot sauce and quickly scoop up a spoonful, blowing several times before testing it.

I need out, Jill. You say after several bites.

Well, get out. Where else do you want to go?

I don't know. I just don't want to be stuck here anymore.

Everyplace gets small. I take another piece of bread and dip it in your gumbo.

Well, I'm ready for someplace else to start to get small, then. You return your attention to your Cajun dish.

I can't help but think this is mostly because of a certain two pieces of mail. I inquire, tearing off another piece of bread. *I mean everyone suffers frustration at work, no matter what they do.*

I have to come back from the almost dead somehow. And I can't think of a better way to save myself than to stop trying to save other people. Actually, I can't think of any other way.

It's necessary for each of us to recognize what's important. But we have to do more than recognize it. We have to figure out how to live it. Most people cheat themselves out of the very things they need the most, even if they know they need them. I've heard you complain about the law for as long as I've known you.

I want to make sure you are serious. If you are, there's no turning back. When we decide to change our lives, we set in motion a landslide. We call into play universal forces and if we don't follow through, we might be run over by the avalanche. I want to be sure you're ready for that before I become one of those forces pushing you through the next doorway. But if you say you're ready, then get behind the wheel. I'll take position behind the bumper and prepare to push.

Okay then, since you brought up childhood dreams, have you ever heard of the idea that you can control your dreams? That instead of being at the mercy of whatever night visions might come, you can actually determine before you go to bed what you will dream about. I ask.

What, like using the Jedi mind trick? A little bit of drink-infused sarcasm.

You could think of it like that. But if this is really what you want, then you have to get serious about it. Fix a picture of it in your mind of where you want to go and don't look back.

You're right, I need to stop talking about it and do it. I know it's the best decision I'll ever make. So, why am I so afraid of making it?

I suspect you're thinking of Christophe and your tendency to give up on love. But it could be more, your pride could be at stake.

I think you're afraid that changing your source of income says something negative about you. The thing is, people stay in jobs too long just like they stay in bad relationships too long. But there's no rule that says you have to. As a matter of fact, as conventional as our society is, people who make major life changes are often celebrated as courageous heroes. I study your face to see if my intuition is on.

But that's only if they're able to do it with a measure of success. You point out. *Until then, society discourages it, frowns upon it, considers it an inability to adjust. Stability is more important. Sacrifice is more noble.* You complain, in between bites, not quite taking time to swallow.

The ego is important, Maggie. It keeps a roof over our heads, food in our stomachs. But if the ego is left to run the whole show, we'll starve to death in other ways. Look at nature. All life is fluid in nature. Stagnation is uniquely human.

Are you saying my butt's gotten fat? You say, deadpan.

I think you're feeling a little better. I didn't mean to lay it on so thick, I was just trying to make it stick. Humor is a great way of dealing with life, but sometimes it's also a great way of not dealing with life.

I know you are right. I do, but it's really fucking hard to hold on to that knowing. And to act on it. You explain.

I nod in agreement. There's no arguing with that, but talking about how hard something is just gives us more excuses not to do it, so I decide to turn in a different direction.

Let's say you hit the reset button, what would you do?

You take another bite before answering; then you explain, earnestly, *Funny you asked that. You know how you can have dozens of conversations that you remember almost nothing about? And then—randomly—someone will say something to you that sticks for some reason?*

I nod.

Well, I've been thinking a lot about what you said about wanting life to be like a restaurant. I don't know why, but that phase has been tumbling around in my brain since then. You consider your soup again before finishing the thought. *Then it dawned on me on the way over here a few nights ago: This is the only place I really feel at home. Not in court, not sitting behind a computer. I don't want to be enmeshed in the tragedies of other people's lives anymore. I want to be part of their celebrations.*

That's the most sober thing I've heard you say all night. *Ever work in a restaurant?*

No, never. You motion with your hand to your bowl.

Might ruin it for you, you know. I mean it's a lot different than eating in one. I take another bread scrap and help myself to the remnants of your dinner.

I'm a quick study. We could start with how to run the bar. I'm already pretty familiar with its contents. You joke again, smiling this time.

First rule is don't drink up the profits. I wink.

Yeah, that might be a hard one. You admit, with a hint of a self-deprecating blush.

I get the feeling that if you were to sell your law books and let those suits get a little dusty, it wouldn't be a problem. I tear another small piece of bread and run it around the inside of the bowl, getting the best of the spices that have fallen to the bottom. When I look up, you're staring at me like a lover trying to work up the courage to have a difficult conversation.

I have a confession. You say, setting your spoon down finally.

Well, it'd be hard to confuse me with a priest, but go ahead, unburden. I lean back from the bar, stand upright and wipe my hands on a bar towel.

I've done a little more than let this idea float through my head. You take the napkin from your lap and wipe your mouth, then set it on the bar next to the empty bowl.

How much more? I toss the bar towel on the sink.

Well, I've been shopping for a building, I contacted a mortgage banker, and I've drafted an ad to sell my books and all my research files. I can tell by your expression you've got your glove open, ready to catch my reaction whichever way it flies.

You weren't kidding. I say, calmly. It takes a couple of seconds for me to register that you used the word "we" earlier. I really haven't put much thought into what my next step would be after *rembrandt* closes its doors. The right thing has always had a way of showing up when I'm ready to move on. Before I can settle on which question to ask first, you add to the surprise.

I've got some equity in my condo I can use, to get us off the ground. You add, the carrot dangling from your words.

And I thought it was going to be me giving you a push into your next life. *Wasn't it you who just said movement is the natural order?* You dare.

No one likes a smart ass. It's my turn to smile.

LOVE: STUDY 10

you and i are love
and love is chaos.
love splinters reality.

love leaves bodies in its wake.
there is no disaster relief fund.
pride is the enemy of love.

love keeps a messy house.
love sleeps on the roof.
love won't come when you call
or call when you come.
love keeps no calendar.
love ignores all boundaries.

love is not loyal or faithful.
obedient or thrifty.
love breaks all rules.

DILLON

You spend the night at my place the night before you take off for India. We stay up late of course, drinking wine and doing our best to ignore the urge to do something irresponsible like sleep together just because we actually get each other.

You tell me you need to find the rhythm of your soul. But I'm pretty sure that's not it. You're more attuned to that sort of thing that ninety percent of the planet. I just think you need to trust it. For all your self-reflection, you have a hell of a time seeing yourself. You're still spending all your time on the riverbank, philosophizing about the movement of water.

I'm pretty sure that love is only an excuse we've made up. Something to justify irrational behavior. Your voice is animated, but your face is stoic.

What if happiness is an illusion. I say. Wouldn't you settle for that?

We talk until early morning, but in conversation, things invariably get left out. The two-way nature of a conversation means that when one person talks, the other tends to forget what they were saying. The only way I know to really sit you down and make sure I say everything I want is to write it down.

That's what I do, then. I write a letter and I slip it into a pocket in your backpack. Hopefully you'll find it before you come home.

Dillon,

I'm not sure I understand life or love. Perhaps no one does.

Sometimes. If we are lucky. If we are really lucky, we get something. Something indefinable finds its way to us. A feeling. Something that lifts us. Something to look forward to. A smile that can't be hidden.

It almost never comes in the packaging we expect. It doesn't wear a watch, and it can't be scheduled.

Everything. Everything depends on how we treat that something. And what we do with it. For something so powerful, it is impossibly fragile. There are a million and eleven things that can kill it. Most of them questions.

Tread too lightly and it may become restless and bored. Seek purchase in another field. Feed it. Sir its coals, fan the flame. And it may burn out of control. Consuming us and it all at once. We must be neither too careful nor too careless. And this is almost impossible.

It has a life. An identity all its own. Different from yours. Inseparable. Not the same as your life. But indistinguishable.

In the end, you have a box of crayons. And it has a white surface.

Whatever you do, don't just sit there.

Love,

Jillian

THE PAINTER

The painter dreamt of drowning. Of two ships colliding. At first it seemed as if the two great vessels would just bounce off one another—like canoes in a river. But then the pointed bow of the other ship rammed through the side of the painter's, breaking windows and ripping through metal.

Within seconds, the ship was taking on water and descending rapidly into the unknown depths. As the ocean rushed in through the windows, the painter was resigned to his fate. There was no thought of escape or rescue.

As he went under, he didn't struggle. Instead, he purposefully took in a large breath of water. There was no pain, no struggle, no gasping. For an instant it seemed that he could actually breathe the fluid in his lungs. That he was one with the water.

Then there was nothing left except the waiting. Waiting for the darkness to embrace the light. And a faint wonder as to where he would awake.

Thomas Lloyd Qualls is a writer, a condition that is apparently incurable. He is also a storyteller, podcaster, former music festival owner, licensed attorney who has overturned two death sentences, and a one-time vagabond who used to wander the globe with a backpack and three changes of clothes. What he means to say is that he is a human being who, so far, has done all these things. He'll probably do more things not on this list.

The *Midwest Book Review* called *Waking Up at Rembrandt's,* "an impressive debut novel showcasing an undeniably talented and imaginative author." His second novel *Painted Oxen* earned seven literary awards, including the Landmark Prize for Fiction, a Silver Nautilus Award, and the award for Best New Fiction at the American Fiction Awards.

Happiness Is an Imaginary Line in the Sand, his third book, is best described as a portable daily oracle. It is the recipient of two Nautilus awards: a Gold Nautilus and Best in Small Press.

With all his creative work, he seeks to bridge the worlds of literary and spiritual and to blur the lines between what is real and what is imagined. He also strives to create worlds where labels are difficult to affix.

Wayfarer
BOOKS & MAGAZINE